SING ANYWAY

A MOONLIGHTERS NOVELLA

ANITA KELLY

For memories of Chopsticks III, and the friends who let me sing along

And for pop music, which saves me still

1

SAM

ALL MY FRIENDS WERE ASSHOLES.

I tried to leave for the bar later tonight; I really did. I sat around my apartment for as long as possible, snacking on cheesy puffs and watching my cats growl at each other. Garfunkel always antagonized Simon and Simon always played right into it. They were both idiots.

But even after stalling for what felt like forever, I was still the first one at Moonie's. Like always.

Moonie's was technically The Moonlight Café, although nobody actually called it that. The *café* in particular always tickled me. As if we were conjuring uncomfortable chairs on the sidewalk in Montmartre, sipping tiny cups of espresso and chomping on perfectly flaky croissants. You couldn't get a croissant at Moonie's if you begged on your hands and knees.

Still, I loved Moonie's, in this pure, uncomplicated way, like children loved snow days, or cats loved tiny dots of red light. I loved its not-so-slight seediness, its sticky floors and dreadful food selection, its weird location in the middle of an industrial wasteland section of the city. Moonie's wasn't a place you happened to stumble into during a night out on the town. Moonie's was a place you went to on purpose.

And even though it didn't actually advertise itself as a queer bar, all the queers knew it was Our Place. We all came here on purpose. For some reason. Some cheap liquor, excellent karaoke reason.

What I *didn't* love was having to be the one who saved our table every time, awkwardly thumbing through my phone and nursing a beer until someone else in our group finally decided to show. It was like my friends completely forgot that time we showed up and our entire favorite table —including the tables from the side we always dragged over to make ÜberTable—was taken by a sloppy bachelorette party. It had been a qualified disaster, but apparently I was the only one who cared.

Or perhaps, my friends simply *knew* I was the only one who cared. Hence taking advantage of me always being here early to save our table.

Although, okay. If I was being honest...I was also here this early for my own sake. Because if I wasn't out of the house by 8:30—the time of night I was typically already rolling into my jam jams and gleefully snuggling under my covers to watch YouTube until I passed out—then the probability of me actually leaving the house at all decreased exponentially.

Sometimes, I wondered if I'd gotten too old and pathetic for even Moonie's.

But no. I wasn't. Not yet. Because I was here now. And each time I came here, it reminded me, reassured me. That I still had the ability to break loose a little. And I needed that.

After tossing my jacket around a chair, I walked to the bar on the opposite side of the room, waited for the super unfriendly butch bartender to notice me. She was here almost every time we came to Moonie's and had never smiled at me once. I was equal parts terrified of and deeply in love with her.

My phone buzzed in my pocket.

Claire: *Harry just vommed all over the nice rug*
Kort: *truly disgusting*
Claire: *going to have to cancel the sitter*
Kort: *ugh, why are babies*
Claire: *I'm so sorry :(*
Kort: *we made poor life choices*

"You need something?"

I jumped. Fuck. Scary Butch Bartender finally noticed me while I was oblivious on my phone, which definitely meant she hated me even more now. This was an ominous start to the evening.

"Sorry, I'm so sorry. Just a Rainier."

She plopped the can on the counter and wordlessly stuck out her hand for my card. After I handed it over with what I hoped was my most charming, so-sorry-again, I-am-gonna-tip-you-so-hard smile, I slinked back to our table. Well, *my* table, currently. Should I make ÜberTable now, to make sure we had it? Except…with Claire and Kort out, that meant their weird neighbors likely wouldn't come, either, which sucked, because even though they were *fucking weird*, they reliably provided at least half of our most memorable Moonie's moments.

With a groan, I remembered Nate was out of town, too. So he and whatever randoms he normally pulled in were also out.

We might not even have to shove an obnoxious number of tables together at all.

I slumped down into my seat at my singular table, accompanied by my cold can of lager and my friend, Instagram. Which I definitely had already caught up on while I was eating cheesy puffs in my apartment.

Sigh. Twitter it was.

Things only began to look up when Kiki, the karaoke jockey, walked by on her way to her station fifteen minutes later and gave me a wave. I smiled back. Kiki was without a doubt our favorite KJ. She liked us, didn't let the same people hog the mic over and over, and was cute as hell. I was pissed Claire and Kort were missing out on a Kiki night. Their loss for deciding to raise spawn.

I'd finished off my Rainier by the time another text of doom appeared on my phone, this time from Rae: *I am so sorry, if I don't get this brief done this weekend I am royally screwed.*

So. Claire, Kort, Weird Neighbors, Nate, Nate's Randoms, *and* Rae were officially missing out on a Kiki night.

I stared at the sparkly letters that adorned the wall next to me, that had adorned this wall for all of eternity: *HAPPY BIRTH AY*, they shouted, seemingly at anyone, the *D* long missing. At Moonie's, every day was someone's birth ay. It had become a phrase of affection amongst my friends and me, particularly at the drunken end of a karaoke night, shouting it at each other nonsensically: HAAAPPY BIRTH-AYYYY!

But clearly, the likelihood of *birth ay* proclamations tonight appeared dim. With everyone else out, the only friends who remained were Steve, whom I loved but who refused to sing at karaoke, which lessened the fun a bit, and Kelsey. And you truly never knew if Kelsey was going to ever actually show to an event or not. Which would be annoying with anyone else, but Kelsey was so fucking hysterical whenever she did decide to show that her flakiness was instantly forgiven every time.

Even if she *did* show tonight, me, Kelsey, and Steve would be...kind of an odd group. Missing too much of the glue of everyone else. Best to bail now for the good of the order.

I stood, moving toward the bar. Man, Butch Bartender was gonna be pissed when I closed out on a $4 tab.

But then the door opened.

I was already at the bar when she walked in. I sucked in a breath.

Lemon yellow dress tonight, splashed all over with large, blood-red poppies. Her shoulders were draped in a velvet jacket the same shade of red as the flowers on her dress. Although the jacket didn't hide the neckline of said dress, which dipped low in a glorious V, framing her breasts perfectly. She laughed as her group walked to their table, and I caught a bright, brief glimpse of it—straight white teeth framed by cherry red lipstick, curving around an exhalation of mirth—before she turned away. She was wearing thick hoop earrings, sea green, just enough of a color contrast to the rest of her outfit to look clever. When she turned, I could see glitter on her cheeks, sparkling gold even under the dim lights.

She always looked good.

But fuck, she looked good tonight.

"Another?"

Butch Bartender had caught me unawares *again*. And when she held up another sweating can of Rainier, I nodded. Like the miserable human being I was.

I scooted back to my table, telling myself it was *not* super creepy to nurse another beer for the sole purpose of getting to hear my karaoke crush sing her signature opening song. I mean, I *did* put on pants and everything for this outing. It would be sad if I left before I even heard one song. Especially if it was hers.

My karaoke crush, or KC as I called her in my head—being that my brain always forgot her actual name, being that we had never actually talked to each other—and her group of friends weren't here *every* time our group was, but like a lot of other Moonie's regulars, we frequently over-lapped. When she didn't show, I had a rotation of other karaoke crushes amongst the Moonie's Strangers Who Didn't Necessarily Feel Like Strangers When We Were Here, as I had a rotation of crushes for almost every aspect of my life.

I was very good at being thirsty. Less successful at the actual drinking part.

Everyone else paled in comparison to my #1 KC, though. She always wore the prettiest clothes, usually brightly colored dresses, as she was tonight. Sometimes she mixed it up, though. Last summer, during a particularly rough heat wave, she came to Moonie's wearing short over-alls in this wacky checkered pattern over a tight tank top. I had never seen her show that much arm or leg before, and she looked so powerful on the dance floor when she sang that I almost passed out.

Because that's what #1 KC was: powerful. I'd over-heard her chatting at her table with her friends before, and her speaking voice was surprisingly feather light and high pitched. But when she had a mic in front of her, she had one of those voices that you could tell came straight from her gut. Like the strength of her lungs could blow, blow, blow your house down. She didn't prance around the dance floor like some of these queers did—although to be clear, I was always here for a prancing queer—but moved her body in a way that mattered, in a way that made you stop and pay attention. She was big and gorgeous and whenever she sang I wanted to just...melt into her.

And then sneak into the bathroom with her and bang against the wall.

Not that that would ever happen.

But a non-binary-person-who-appeared-to-have-no-friends could dream.

Aaaand there she went. Walking up to Kiki. Putting in her first request.

I took a big swig of Rainier. Which I then proceeded to choke on. The bar was starting to fill up now, and not only was I taking up a whole table by myself, I was apparently losing the ability to even function properly.

I got a hold of myself, and moved to a small two-seater, back in the corner. As far from ÜberTable as I could get. Such was my fate.

My phone buzzed in my pocket again.

Text from Steve: *wait so is anyone making it to Moonie's tonight?? Running super late anyway, let me know!*

Kiki picked up the mic and moved to the center of the floor.

"Time to get this party started, my people! My request list is still pretty light, and you know it won't be that way for long. Bring me your songs, babes!"

With a wink, she launched into the first song of the night.

Kiki liked to kick off karaoke herself, which, considering she was going to spend the next several hours of her life listening to drunk people screech and holler in her ear, she fully deserved. She had a great voice, a cute little shimmy, and she always chose the best throwbacks.

Although when she launched into Jennifer Paige's classic 1998 hit, "Crush"—which I would have appreciated

7

on any other night, because, hilarious—I nearly thwacked my forehead onto the table.

Instead, I steadfastly stared around at the rest of the room, only glancing at the back of my #1 KC's head for the briefest of moments, telling myself Jennifer was right. It was just a little crush. Not like I fainted every time we touched. Not that we had ever touched. So perhaps the jury was still out on that one.

And then Kiki was back behind her little table, and shouting into the mic: "Here we go, everybody! Put your hands together for crowd favorite, Lilyyyyy!"

#1 KC—*Lily*, how did I always forget that, so pretty—got up from her table. She walked over to Kiki with a smile and took the mic. Her yellow dress swished.

And I couldn't tell if I was excited, or if I was sad. Excited, because it was going to be awesome. Sad, because once Lily sang Carrie Underwood, Kiki would let a bunch of other losers sing until she gave Lily another round. Which meant that after this, I'd truly have no excuse to be here anymore. And dammit, coming all the way out to Moonie's without getting to have a true Moonie's night was a disappointment of epic proportions.

But then Lily opened her mouth.

And okay, maybe the awesomeness beat out the disappointment. Even though I'd heard Lily sing "Before He Cheats" at least ten times before, it still kicked me in the gut as soon as she started.

I never knew what she'd end up singing later on, but every single time she was here, Lily started the night with "Before He Cheats." And I admired the hell out of it every single time, because I had to be at least six drinks in to even think about approaching a microphone, and even then, only when one of my friends dragged me with them. But to be one of the first singers of the night meant putting yourself out there to a half-full room of sober people. And it wasn't like Lily chose an easy one to start with, like a Lisa Loeb "Stay" kind of selection, one you could quietly croon while everyone else got their cheap drinks and shitty fries and ignored you.

No, Lily chose this bluesy, shit-eating country song with a chorus that used up entire lungfuls of air. It was like she needed to launch herself into this balls-to-the-wall song to get herself into the groove. Because she was a little hesitant at first, a little shaky during that very first *right now* of the opening verse. But soon she was *belting* it, leaning over when she got real into the best lines, swaying her hips across the floor during the sassy verses, and Jesus. What a star. By the end, her eyes would be sparkling, and everyone in the room would be a little bit in love with her.

Or maybe it was just me. But seriously, every time she sang about scratching her keys into the side of that dude's car—well, I wouldn't have minded if she wanted to carve her name into *my* leather seats. Or whatever. I would be one hundred percent down with whatever the fuck she wanted to do, was what I was saying.

And while I always felt this way, there was something about watching her sing tonight while I sat here alone that made the whole experience heightened. The table next to me had filled up with a bunch of people I didn't recognize, and they were all chatting loudly with each other like Lily wasn't singing "Before He Cheats," and I sort of wanted to bash their heads in. Even though Past Me had probably chatted with my friends too during "Before He Cheats." Because it was a bar, and that was what you did. And you weren't drunk enough yet to loudly shout along with every dumb song every stranger chose to sing.

But Present Me had literally nothing else to do except stare and listen to every word of it. And fuck me, but it felt

9

like Lily was singing directly to me. And it was magnificent. Every hair on my body stood on end.

Except. Maybe Lily *was* singing directly to me.

Because suddenly, that was what was happening.

My karaoke crush was staring back.

2

LILY & SAM

THEY WERE ALONE TONIGHT, which was odd. Maybe that was what made my eyes snag onto theirs, the surprise of their solitude, and their eyes so intent on mine. I had felt their eyes on me before, of course—I was good at this, and I'd always gotten the sense from the way they watched, from the enthusiasm of their applause after I finished a song, that they knew I was good at this, too.

And even if you knew you were good at something, it felt fucking satisfying to have a stranger acknowledge it.

But why were they all by their lonesome at that little table in the corner tonight? They—and I was pretty sure they used they, because sometimes they wore a black jean jacket with a *they/them* pin on it—often seemed to be the first one here of their group, but eventually their friends would join them. I liked their group; it felt like theirs and ours had this unspoken Moonie's camaraderie. We cheered and danced for each other's songs, respected each other's favorite tables if one group got here first.

But I had always secretly found this stranger, the one currently sitting alone in a corner, to be particularly adorable. They seemed shy; never sang by themselves, always dragged up with one of their friends later in the night. And even then, they refused to look at the crowd, staring only at their friends as they shuffled awkwardly around the dance floor with one hand in their pockets, grinning. Having fun but embarrassed, face flushed bright red. I always wanted to run up to them afterward and squeeze their cheeks.

And then maybe squeeze their ass, if they let me, just to see how they'd react.

They also consistently knew the songs, which I respected. That was the thing about karaoke: everyone thought they were safe throwing any song up, since the words were right there on the screen in front of you. But if you didn't *really* know the lyrics, the beats to come in on, the rhythm of the lines—you were screwed.

Cutie in the Corner didn't have a great voice, and might have blushed and shuffled while they sang, but they always knew the words.

When I caught their eye tonight, though, their face wasn't red, and they weren't grinning. They were...looking at me like I was the only one in the room, eyes dark and serious.

And I was almost done with the song, so the claws of Carrie's confidence were firmly implanted now. I felt sexy and strong and *good*. And their eyes on me felt right. Like maybe everyone else in the room were the real idiots, for not looking at me like that. And so I kept staring back.

And, well, damn. Singing at Moonie's was always a bit of a rush, but maintaining eye contact with a stranger while I did it was...was...kind of hot. And really fucking intense.

I kept thinking they'd look away. Or that I would. But I found I couldn't. Or didn't want to. Or both.

The Power of Carrie must have been strong tonight. Because while they looked at me, and I sang about getting my revenge, it almost felt real. Like I could be a star. Like I had someone waiting for me in the crowd who thought I could be a star, too.

By the end of the song, my heart was fluttering around in my chest in this hectic pitter patter, and I felt hot all over.

When I handed Kiki back the mic, my hand was shaking.

Quickly, I wiped my palm on my dress. I took a deep breath.

And I turned around and walked right past my table— oh god, my friends were going to give me so much shit— and headed straight back there to that sad little corner, and the stranger who had just made me feel sexy as hell. Because it was Saturday night. And it was Moonie's. It didn't matter if I made a fool of myself. It was safe.

I watched their eyes grow wide as I plunked myself down in the seat across from them. They looked slightly petrified, which was real stinking cute. And helped me feel a little more normal. Because some of the heat that had flared in me while I was singing cooled when I realized I was back to wanting to pinch their cheeks. Which was probably good.

"Hey," I said. "Do you mind if I sit out that embarrassing post-singing high here with you for a second? You know, when you have to go back to your table after a song and suddenly don't want anyone to look at you ever again so you have to pretend to act chill even though you're not?"

Their mouth only gaped for a second. And then they blinked and appeared to get control of themselves.

"Oh my god," they said. "You should never feel embarrassed. You are *amazing*."

I bit my lip to keep myself from smiling too hard. Why had I never talked to this person before? I should have them on speed dial for whenever I needed a boost, back in the non-Moonie's real world.

Because the truth of the matter was, I *wasn't* a star. Or *amazing*. At least not in that breathless way they had said it. I was as shy as Adorable Blusher here appeared, most of the time. Or maybe shy wasn't the right word. When I applied it to myself, *shy* made me feel like a little kid. I was introverted. Quiet. Which was fine; that was who I was and how I was comfortable.

It was only when a KJ handed me a mic, and all I felt was the warmth of the lights and the dark comfort of this bar, which only ever seemed to be full of queers and freaks —my people—that I got to be...something different.

"Thank you." I cleared my throat, wishing now that I had stopped at my table to get my drink. I always needed a few good, strong swigs after Carrie. "Where are your friends tonight?"

"All bailed," they said on a sigh, seeming to relax a little. "Which would have been nice to know *before* I left the house, but, oh well."

They shook a lock of hair off their forehead. It was dark, almost black, streaked through with grey and on the curly side, perpetually disheveled. They were wearing a plain black t-shirt tonight, with a turquoise pocket. It was a smart pop of color. It also highlighted their eyes, which were blue-ish-green and...rather spectacular. Which I had always suspected was the case. But it was pleasant, seeing the evidence up close as they glanced across the table at me. They looked a bit older, their skin a bit weathered, the stubble adorning their chin flecked with grey, just like their hair. But those eyes were pretty as sin. And made all the better, I thought, by the fact that either they wore mascara or had the prettiest eyelashes known to humanity. But I was pretty sure it was mascara. Because sometimes they sported eyeliner, too, some shadow on their lids. Tonight, though, it was all lashes.

It occurred to me that, once again, we had probably been staring at each other for too long.

"I'm Lily, by the way," my brain finally kicked into gear to say.

"Right! Sorry. I'm Sam." Apologizing for no reason. *Sam.* Adorbs.

"Do you want to sit with us?" I offered with a tilt of my head, back toward our table. "You don't have to. But you can if you want."

"I—" They opened their mouth. Closed it. And then, instead of answering my question, blurted: "I like your dress."

"Oh!" I looked down at myself, as if I had forgotten what I was wearing. "Thank you. It's one of my more recent favorites. I was pretty happy with how it turned out."

Understatement. I was thrilled with how it had turned out. Like after years of working at it, I was finally starting to understand draping. And how to actually shape fabric to my hips properly.

"Wait." Sam's eyebrows furrowed. "You made that?"

"I did. Making clothes is…" I waved a hand around. *My dream.* "Kind of a hobby. It's surprisingly satisfying, making your own clothes. Especially when you're fat, and shopping for store bought stuff is such a nightmare."

"So you make most of your clothes?" Sam asked, brows still in a cute bunch, and I appreciated it, that they didn't react to the f-word, that they didn't try to tell me I was wrong.

I nodded, and they leaned back in their chair, shaking their head.

"That's...incredible. Your clothes are always so great. That's not a hobby; that's like...a fucking *skill*."

Your clothes are always so great. Like they had noticed them before.

"God," I couldn't help but laugh. "Can I just carry you around in my pocket all the time so you can keep showering me with compliments whenever I need them?"

"Yes," Sam said immediately.

And then blushed.

I was fucking glad I had come to this table.

"Uh," they said, looking away and scratching at the back of their neck. "Can I, um. Get you a drink?"

"Sure." I had a barely-drunk drink back at our table, but I was not going to object to a person who thought I was awesome getting me another one. "Gin and tonic?"

"Cool." And then they were gone, *wooshing* over to the bar Wile E. Coyote style.

I sprinted back to our table to down my already-purchased G&T in one gulp.

"*Lily!*" Preeti hissed, eyes wide, leaning over the table. "Tell me everything."

"Yeah, what the hell?" Jonny smacked my arm. "You walked right on past us like you didn't even know us. And the way you two were eye-fucking when you were up there! I didn't even know you knew that dude!"

"I love this." Bri pointed her beer bottle at me. "Y'all know Lily being bold at karaoke is literally my favorite thing in the world. I have a good feeling about this. It's gonna be a good night."

And just like that, the ridiculously large gulp of alcohol I'd swallowed down sloshed uneasily around my insides.

The Power of Carrie *had* been too strong. I had overestimated. Because the *amazing* person Sam thought I was— who plopped themselves at a table, uninvited, to talk to a stranger—wasn't actually me. *Lily being bold at karaoke.* Sam had been flirting with an illusion.

And now...the idea of keeping up that illusion with Sam for only a few hours, knowing it would have to end at last call, only seemed depressing.

I didn't know what I had been thinking. I *hadn't* been thinking, was the issue. Blasted karaoke adrenaline.

"I *don't* know them," I finally said, when I realized all my friends were staring expectantly at me. "And don't call them dude. At least, I don't think." I glanced over at the bar, where the bartender was sliding two G&Ts into Sam's hands. I took another deep breath, trying to shake off the icky feeling creeping into my brain, threatening to send the Power of Carrie toppling.

This was fine. We hadn't *eye fucked*. They just didn't deserve to sit by themselves all night. This was good. A totally normal thing. There was nothing wrong with keeping up the illusion of Karaoke Lily for a few hours of letting loose and getting to know another Moonie's regular a little better. I was being dramatic.

"I'm pretty sure they use they/them, and their name is Sam, and their friends all bailed at the last minute, and they like my dress—" *okay*, I didn't have to mention that part, but they had been so nice about the dress— "and I invited them to sit with us, so just be fucking cool or I'll kill you in your sleep. Hey!"

I smiled brightly up at Sam, who was standing uncertainly at the end of the table. I patted the empty chair to my right. Friendly. Bold. Moonie's normal. "Sam, meet everyone. Everyone, meet Sam."

OH GOD. I had been mildly okay with Lily coming over to talk to me—HAHA JOKES, it had been fucking wild, but once the actual talking started it had also been kind of fun. I think.

But being thrown straight into meeting a whole new group of people—even if, sure, they were all people I'd seen do karaoke a bunch of times before, which was such a ridiculous, vulnerable act that we probably rated as acquaintances, at least, maybe—was upping the ante. It was hard not to feel pathetic for real, like the only reason they were inviting me into their club was because my friends had abandoned me. Because...that was the only reason they were inviting me into their club.

I sat down and slid Lily her gin and tonic. I hoped she didn't like fancy gin. Butch Bartender had raised her eyebrows at me, being that I'd never ordered a gin and tonic before, and asked "Well liquor okay?" And I had no idea what even constituted good gin so I'd just nodded. Although, wait, the pretty blue bottle I often stared at while waiting for Butch Bartender to take pity on me was gin, I was pretty sure. Dammit. I should have gotten Lily the pretty blue gin.

"Happy to have you, Sam! I'm Bri." A Black woman with a wide smile reached her hand out to me across the table. "Sorry to hear about your friends. I always love watching that short one do Bel Biv Devoe."

"Nate," I smiled. "That's his sole go-to, yeah. He's out of town. My friend Steve might show up later," I checked my phone in my pocket, to make sure I hadn't missed any more texts. "...but probably not."

"What do you do, Sam?" A guy on Lily's other side leaned forward. "Jonny, by the way."

"Hey, Jonny." I gave a dorky little wave across the table, until I realized the extent of its dorkiness and quickly aborted it. "I teach at the university downtown."

Lily turned to me, eyes bright. How did sitting next to someone seem so much more intimate than sitting across from them? It should have been the opposite. But our shoulders were almost brushing now. I could *smell* her here, some kind of citrusy perfume, and I wanted to bathe in it. So much potential for knees knocking into each other. Thighs pressing together, possibly, if I played my cards right.

Which I definitely wouldn't, because my romantic prowess was level negative three.

"You're a professor?"

I took a sip of the G&T, which was not half bad.

"It's not that impressive, I swear. It's more like...a job for people who didn't want to leave college and didn't know what else to do."

"I doubt that's true," Lily said. "Or else colleges would be full of a lot of shitty professors."

"Yeah, well." I shrugged. Case in point.

"What do you teach?" Jonny asked.

"History."

"Oh my god, history was my favorite subject in school!" Another woman at the table shouted. "Do you have, like, a specialty? Professors always study real specific shit."

I shifted in my chair, realizing how long it had been since I'd met anyone new. I wasn't used to talking this much about myself.

"Well, I teach pretty much whatever they tell me to teach, but...my research focuses mainly on early 20th century America. Immigration in early 20th century America, specifically."

"Oh yeah," the woman who loved history nodded her head approvingly. "That's sexy shit."

"Is it?" I laughed. "I find it rather upsetting and discriminatory, actually."

"No, Preeti means the fact that you study it," Lily filled in. "You do *research*. That," she lifted her glass, "is sexy."

I was pretty sure Preeti and Lily were fucking with me. There was nothing remotely sexy about me, including my research. From my already-meticulously-studied chosen field to my physique, which could best be described as *chunky*, everything about me screamed *mediocre white person*. I had been told I had nice eyes, a point which I could concede, but I failed at pretty much everything else: hair product, originality, fashion choices. God, I *wished* I could make clothes that actually made sense for my body, like Lily. Or even understood how to shop for them.

I lived alone in a small apartment with two cats and more maps than any single person would ever have a tangible use for. I lacked interesting hobbies.

The only vaguely interesting thing about me was a late in life acceptance of Feeling Real Weird About Gender. And even then, *interesting* wasn't exactly the right word. I had no idea what the right word was, and had been searching for the last few years to find it. I'd take an even remotely accurate string of words at this point. But when I did find them, I'd buy a new sparkly journal in celebration.

And maybe after writing those close-enough-to-accurate words down in fancy pen on every single page, my brain would finally be able to shut up about it.

Or maybe the journal wouldn't be sparkly. Maybe it'd be a nice matte gray.

It would depend on the day, really.

"It's...no," I managed to get out, unsure about whether I should explain that half of my life was trying to get undergrads to think past the beliefs their parents had taught them and utterly failing. And grading the same papers over and over. And feeling like a tool whenever I had to meet with like, actual smart people.

Or maybe I should've just gone with the whole Lily-thinking-I'm-sexy point of view.

"What do your students call you?" she asked. "Professor...?"

"Bell," I said. "But I usually ask that they just call me Sam, because Professor Bell feels weird. Even though whenever I ask them to call me Sam, there's normally at least a quarter of the class that look at me like they *know* I am wasting their too-expensive tuition, and they...are not wrong, probably. Anyway!" Wow, apparently my brain really couldn't go with the *pretend you're sexy* plan there. Probably for the best. "What do you all do? You know," I cast a glance at Lily, "when you're not singing and designing your own clothes, and stuff."

"We all work together, actually," Lily said, gesturing toward the rest of the table. But she totally smiled at me first, quick and small, like it was a secret. "At a veterinary clinic. Bri's one of our vets, and Jonny and Preeti are vet techs. I'm a lowly receptionist."

"Excuse me," Preeti butted in. "I think you mean to say customer care specialist."

Lily rolled her eyes. "Sure."

"Seriously, though," Bri took a swig of her beer. "Lily's job is harder than mine."

"Bri," Lily deadpanned. "You literally took out a dog's eyeball today."

"Yeah, and then I got to kill some old lady's cat and she cried for an hour. It's a job that keeps on giving, veterinary medicine. But *you* had to deal with that asshole who made that other client cry in the lobby. And who then tried to refuse to pay for bloodwork. Even though he definitely fucking okayed the bloodwork. Anyway, you're a goddamn angel."

"One hundred percent," Jonny said.

I agreed that Lily was probably an angel. But I hated that she had to deal with assholes, instead of...being surrounded by pretty fabric all day, or whatever she actually wanted to do with her life. I had to fight a completely inappropriate urge to rub my hand over her back.

"*Anyway,*" Lily said pointedly, "Some other people will likely show up in a bit. We do have some friends outside of work."

"Debatable. But yeah, my roommate Alexis will probably show up at some point," Preeti said. "And Jonny's new boyfriend that he won't tell us anything about."

"I don't even know if he's coming, and if you call him my boyfriend, I will punch you in the face."

"Wow, y'all are *feisty* tonight." Bri raised her eyebrows.

"And up next at the mic, we have Preeti and Bri!"

Preeti squealed and raised her hands in the air.

"Dammit, Preeti, what did you put my name on?" Bri slammed down the last of her beer as she stood. "I am not nearly drunk enough for this shit yet."

"You'll like it. Come on." Preeti dragged her by the arm over to Kiki.

I was close enough—Lily and her friends' table was the one closest to the dance floor—to hear Bri mutter "motherfucker" when the song came up on the screen. But she lifted the mic to her mouth to say, "You better fucking let me do the Monica part."

Preeti only had time to roll her eyes, as if this was clearly already established, and then they were launching into "The Boy is Mine."

Lily was leaning forward to support her friends, elbows on the table, but her shoulders immediately began to bounce to the beat. Her hair, dyed platinum blonde, was up in two tight knots on either side of her head. Up close, I could see how neat the part was, her dark roots exposed at the perfectly symmetrical line. I pictured her getting ready for tonight in whatever her apartment—house?—looked like, sitting in front of a mirror, running a comb expertly down her scalp. It made a shiver run all the way down to my toes.

I took another sip of gin & tonic.

And even though the night still felt early, apparently two Rainiers and a G&T were enough to loosen me up. Because when Lily looked over her shoulder at me, her chair dancing having gotten even more pronounced as the song progressed, I somehow found it in me to lip sync at her, with a bit of flair, "I know it's killing you inside," and she smiled.

Not a secret smile like before. A thrilled, mouth cracked wide open, *I approve* smile.

Against all odds, it was possible this night out at Moonie's wasn't going to be a total failure after all.

3

LILY & SAM

SHORTLY AFTER BRI and Preeti sat back down, and Jonny's new boyfriend showed up—his name was Pablo and he *kissed Jonny on the cheek* when he walked in—I spotted that the table next to us finally seemed to have abandoned The Binder. And before they could protest, I darted over and grabbed it.

Moonie's karaoke system had nearly every song you could think of, but even though we'd been doing this for years, I still liked a good perusal through The Binder for inspiration. They also had a database of songs you could search through on this ancient laptop in the corner, but it was like, *dude you got a Dell* old. The Binder was the best.

"Here's what I'm thinking," I said to Sam, plopping it down on the table between us. "We should do something totally cheesy and classic, because we don't know each other's tastes well enough yet to choose something else."

Their eyes widened comically, as they had when they saw me approach their table. I loved it just as much this time.

"Oh," they said, sitting up. "You mean, like, singing together?"

"Obviously," I said. "Obviously we are singing together."

Their mouth formed a little O.

"You…" they scratched their forehead. "Maybe you don't remember my singing abilities, from previous karaoke nights?"

"Oh, I do," I smiled. "I know you can't sing. But I also know this is Moonie's, and it doesn't matter. And you only sing when someone else makes you, so this is me, making you."

They grimaced.

"So…something totally cheesy and classic?"

"Yes!" I beamed. "Except not like, horrifying cheesy and classic. No 'I Will Survive' or 'Pour Some Sugar On Me' or whatever."

"Oh god," Sam said. "That guy who always does 'Pour Some Sugar On Me.'"

"I know; he's the worst. But maybe like…Aretha? Or Celine. Oh, or Stevie?"

Sam shrugged.

"I've done Stevie before. Are we talking 'Superstition' or like, 'Sir Duke' territory?"

"Wait." I stopped on a page, stuck my finger on the sticky lamination. "We can do Stevie later, maybe, but *obviously*, we should start with this."

Sam leaned closer—some hair fell over their forehead —and then they started to laugh. I was obsessed with their laugh. I remembered hearing it vibrating across the room from their table in the past—my second favorite thing about them, behind their karaoke shuffle dance—but having it rumble right in my ear filled my veins with pleasure. It was a laugh that was half hiccup, half snort. It was deeply unattractive and strangely made me want to kiss them.

"Lily. That is probably the most cliché karaoke song of all time."

"But for good reason!" I protested. "It's still enjoyable, every single time! And it's so fun to sing." I poked them in the leg. "Come on."

They were still shaking their head, arms crossed over their chest. "Fine," they said, but their eyes were laughing. "Whatever."

I practically ran the slip of paper to Kiki.

LILY WAS ONLY BACK in her seat for thirty seconds before Kiki called her name again. For a panicked second, I thought she was sending us up right away for the song Lily had just given her, the song request slip that, improbably, had my name next to hers. But it wasn't; it was another request Lily had put in earlier. It was "Today" by the Smashing Pumpkins.

And it was...damn. I liked hearing Lily sing "Before He Cheats" for the pure fun, turn-me-on factor, but this was different. Lily's voice, like Billy Corgan's, somehow went from light and sweet to dark and gritty in the matter of a breath. This song was all fuzzy guitar and irrepressible energy, optimistic and bittersweet all at once, and halfway through I was already half-hard, just sitting there and watching her. My chest felt weirdly full of...happiness, maybe.

But I completely forgot that toward the end of the song, Billy sings *I want to turn you on* over and over. And this time, when the words came out of Lily's mouth, a delicious growl, she didn't lock eyes with me like before. She merely glanced at me once and away. But that glance was enough to make my throat dry.

That glance was enough to make me wonder what the hell I was doing.

Was this simply all in my head? Were her insides also churning when she sang *I want to turn you on* and looked at me? Because it was suddenly clear I was out of my depth here. Sitting at this table was the most impulsive thing I had done in...my life?

She was the one who came to me. So maybe impulsive wasn't the right word, since I was pretty much dragged into this situation, albeit willingly. Maybe this was normal for her, or her friends? Maybe they dragged strangers into their lives all the time?

But it struck me very deeply at that moment, surrounded by that table of almost-acquaintances, watching Lily on the dance floor—a Lily who knew my name, who looked at me when she sang tonight, and not just on accident—that it wasn't normal for me.

What was the endgame here? Were we just going to sing together, and drink together, and say goodbye? And then the next time we were both at Moonie's again we could laugh and hug and say, 'Hey! How've you been?' That sounded nice. Normal-ish, maybe, for people who were better at socializing than me, who didn't hang out with the same core group of people they'd known since college and no one else.

Or were Lily and I going to end the night with one of us straddling the other's lap, our tongues in each other's mouths? That seemed like a very un-me, not-normal possibility—my tongue hadn't been in anyone's mouth since Dan, and after Dan, I seriously contemplated whether the muscle should remain safe and sound inside my own body for the rest of my life, and had landed pretty firmly on *yes*.

But yet, it was becoming increasingly difficult to *not* picture that happening with Lily and me. Which was...exciting, obviously. And terrifying.

I knew I was veering into serious overthinking territory here. But the thing was, it wasn't just romantic prowess I lacked. Dan had highlighted in a particularly painful way how bad I was at relationships, but he came at the tail end of several decades' worth of failed relationships. I either wanted the wrong things, or wanted too much.

And so over the last year, I had decided to turn *wanting* into a game. Because I was tired. I felt committed now to wanting in a way that was safe: silently watching Lily at Moonie's all those previous nights of the last few years. Finding quiet, luxurious joy in the mornings when my favorite barista was on shift, pulling my espresso shots with those perfectly toned, artistically tattooed forearms. Understanding that my station in life wasn't likely to change at this point in the game, that I would keep teaching undergrads who seemed increasingly far away from my own life experiences with each passing year, until I could one day retire and wile away my time watching travel documentaries about places I would never be able to go.

But it didn't feel sad, necessarily. Sometimes the wanting felt like enough. Wanting gave you things to look forward to. I looked forward to Pretty Barista's forearms, to the lightning flashes of possibility at Moonie's. Thirst was a perfectly good reason to wake up every day, in my estimation. It was when you thought you actually had the things you wanted that the future loomed with inevitable disappointment and devastation. I was too old for all of that now.

But somehow, by accident, I was here. Sharing glances with a woman who made wanting—*real* wanting, a visceral escalation of quiet, secret wanting—feel easy. Justified. Comfortable and safe, somehow.

Even though the tiny voice of reason that existed somewhere in the recesses of my brain was shouting at me that none of this was safe at all. That I was doing it again. Pretending something was bigger than it was.

By the time Lily flounced back into her seat next to me, I was taking slow, steady breaths through my nose to get myself together. Trying to picture giving her a simple hug goodnight. A friendly greeting the next time we met at Moonie's.

And then she looked at me, and her brown eyes were so bright and alive that my mind went kind of melty and soft. The tiny voice of reason in the soft tissue of my brain was all but extinguished. And without thinking about it, I reached out and ran a finger over her knuckles, resting in her lap.

"Need that minute to get chill again?" I asked. "I can pretend to not want to stare at you, if it helps."

But she shook her head and smiled. "Nah," she said. "I'm good this time."

I should have left then, probably. If I didn't want the lap straddling, tongue stuff to happen. But I didn't. Instead, I stayed long enough until time slid into the blurry karaoke alternate universe. Where all that mattered was each song, singing along and laughing and forgetting that anything other than this—pop songs and nostalgia and queer people—existed.

The first song I somehow allowed myself to be pulled onto the dance floor for was Flo Rida's "Low," which was, both the song itself and the dancing that was happening to it, absolutely ridiculous. There was no real stage at Moonie's, just the open dance floor at the front of the room, so whenever the night hit that spot, that point where all self-consciousness fled and someone chose a song that really popped, half of the room congregated up there, swarming around the singer, one silly, uncoordinated mass that tore down all borders. Including the border that should have prevented Sam Bell from ever, ever dancing to Flo Rida's "Low."

But Lily, of course, *could* get low, like really fucking impressively so, and I just sort of bounced around haphazardly and tried not to get too hard while she worked her hips and her breasts and her shoulders in an exceedingly distracting way. The only thing that saved me from combusting was the fact that there were twenty other assholes around us doing the same exact thing.

Five seconds after "Low," as we were making our way, sweaty and breathing too hard, back to the table, the next singer busted out a Lady Gaga banger that I had definitely not even thought about in at least ten years. Which meant we immediately changed course and charged back to the dance floor.

And then—shockingly, because I had almost forgotten—Kiki called our names. *Lily and Sam.*

And next thing I knew, I had a microphone in my hand, and Lily was beaming at me. And I told myself that this would be the easiest thing I'd ever done because I could let Lily carry us the entire way. But my face flushed red anyway as the words flashed on the screen attached to the ceiling above us: "Total Eclipse of the Heart."

And then the words popped up, and Lily elbowed me in the side and said, "You're Voice 1," and fuck, I *couldn't* just let Lily carry us because this was a duet. Which I would have fully realized when Lily put it down on that slip of paper if I hadn't been so distracted by her face, and the dimples in her round cheeks when she smiled.

I had to sing the dumb "turn around" parts, and my

30

voice cracked on the third or tenth one in—the first one that was followed by "bright eyes," because who can actually hit that pitch? No one, that's who. And Lily—put together, karaoke goddess Lily—actually *giggled* into the mic at me as she tried to get through the first "every now and then I fall apart," and it was so cute that I discovered I wasn't even embarrassed. Or maybe I was just drunk. Either way, it all felt worth it, the very probable humiliation, to be right next to Lily on that dance floor as she sang about powder kegs giving up sparks and really needing me tonight. Or, no, not *me*, per se. Forever was gonna start tonight for *someone*. But I had given myself over to this thing now, and would volunteer as tribute if she asked.

And the thing about duets was that sometimes only singing your lines alone was actually...kind of boring, but you didn't know if it was a faux pas or not to join in on the other person's lines. But toward the end of the song Lily was waving her arms at me in a 'come on' kind of gesture, so that we were both screaming all of those completely over-the-top lyrics together. And it was funny because I'd only ever been up here with a microphone in my hand next to my friends who had known me for decades; had always thought I would only be comfortable doing such a ridiculous thing with them at my side. But I had known Lily for all of a few hours, and somehow it felt the same.

When it was done, the tinkle of the piano accompanying the last "turn around, bright eyes" fading away into the night, that Embarrassing Post-Singing High Lily had mentioned earlier hit me full force. I still wasn't embarrassed, exactly, but I didn't want to break the spell. Didn't want to go back to Lily's table right now and have all of her friends smirk at us.

I put a hand on her elbow as we handed back our mics.

"Drink?" I motioned with my head toward the bar. She nodded.

The actual number of gin and tonics both Lily and I had consumed had grown muddled. I only knew there kept being clear, refreshing drinks on the table garnished with likely completely unsanitary limes, and we kept drinking them. I could also tell, from the woozy way my head felt, especially after singing Bonnie Tyler, and from the way that literally every single thing that was happening seemed perfect and beautiful, that I was approaching my limit.

But I stood at the edge of the bar, elbow brushing Lily's elbow, and ordered one more from Scary Bartender anyway. She raised an eyebrow at me as she handed them over, like she had no idea what Lily was doing with me, and I shrugged. Her guess was as good as mine.

"Tell me more about your clothes," I said before bringing the tiny plastic straw to my mouth and turning my body toward Lily. It was quieter here at the bar, away from the dance floor, and I wanted a chance to breathe, to talk to her more. It was better lit here too, and I could see how her pale skin was flushed with patches of pink, either from the singing or the dancing, down her neck, toward the tops of those lovely breasts. Her hair knots were still firmly in place, but the heat of the now-crowded room had made a few tendrils near her forehead spring loose: small, sweat-soaked curls. And for a second, the wanting became acute: a flash in my veins of wishing she was truly mine.

"You really want to know?" She faced me, an eyebrow raised. "Because once I get going on this topic, I can get kind of...verbose. Or maybe obnoxious is the better word."

"I promise," I smiled. "I am here for your verbosity."

She leaned her back against the bar, elbows propped on the counter.

"Well." She cleared her throat. "It's a well-established

truth that shopping as a 'plus size'—" air quotes, eye roll, "—person is a pain in the ass."

I nodded.

"Most bigger chain stores these days, like Old Navy or whatever, do have plus size options, but they only go up to 3 or 4x, if you're lucky. And even those plus size options aren't available *in store*, only online—as if our existence is too shameful to exist in public, or something—so you can't try them on. So you waste a ton of time and money and guesswork on clothes that might not even fit you well anyway."

She took a sip of her drink, shaking her head.

"Even if you find stores with bigger sizes, it's tough. Because fat people's bodies are so different, you know? Some of us have big bellies and skinny legs. Some have big hips but are skinnier up top. Some of us are short and some of us are tall. And for people with breasts, sometimes nothing seems right. I can't tell you how many dresses I've bought that made my ass look fantastic but were weird flappy bags from my shoulders to my stomach. And like, I have great breasts!" She motioned to her chest. "Work with my breasts, people!"

"Um." I realized too late that these were statements I did not need to respond to. Because Lily looked at me, eyes twinkling with what I hoped was laughter. "Uh. Yes. I agree."

Her mouth curved into a grin. She looked like she was going to say something, but then she schooled her features a bit and faced away from the bar again.

"Anyway. Eventually I was like, my kingdom for an outfit that actually fits my shoulders, my boobs, my stomach, and my hips. So I started messing around on my own. I saved up for my own sewing machine. And...it was hard, and frustrating, when I wasn't an expert designer right from the get-go. But it was also fun. Now that I'm better at it, it's really fun." She paused. "I love wearing this dress. That I made myself, that I feel 100% comfortable in, that makes me feel sexy. But most fat people don't have that, which is so frustrating to me. Society already does enough on its own to make us feel like shit. Having to suffer a lifetime of ill-fitting clothes feels like kicking us when we're already down. I wonder if most people even know what it feels like, to wear something that actually fits them, how it can be...completely transforming. For people who have never had that feeling, clothes feel like this extra burden instead of something that can make them feel amazing."

I was contemplating whether I had ever felt 100% comfortable in an outfit, and coming up with a resounding *nope*, when Lily kept going. But her voice had turned softer, less righteous, and I had to lean in closer to hear.

"Anyway, I think maybe I would have turned to making my clothes anyway, even if I wasn't fat as fuck. My grandma made clothes, too. She was the one who taught me how to sew when I was a kid, even though I was always terrified that her ancient Singer was going to cut off all my fingers."

She smiled, and I felt something in my chest open up, grateful and eager to absorb this precious Lily memory. Like suddenly I was tumbling head over heels into her life in a real way. Like with each second, she was further and further from being a mere karaoke crush.

"Going to the fabric store with her when I was a kid was one of my favorite things, this routine that was just ours. I could have spent hours running my hands over all the different fabrics—silk, all the different kinds of cotton, fleece, denim. Knowing that my grandma could take all of that and make it into something useful. And the button aisle!" Lily turned toward me again, moving a fraction

34

closer, as if she needed to be as close as possible to fully exude the magic of the button aisle. "So many shapes and colors. The fucking best."

She turned away again, taking a sip of her drink, and I felt the loss of her heat.

"When I started thinking about messing around with clothes, when I finally got my own machine, it felt like coming home in a way, you know? It breaks my heart that I started doing it after my grandma died. She didn't like my body," I was watching Lily like a hawk by this point, so I saw the way she swallowed here, thick and slow, "but I think she would have at least respected my clothes."

A silence stretched then. I didn't know what to say. Although my brain had plenty it *wanted* to say to her grandma. If, you know, she wasn't dead.

Eventually, I brushed my fingers over her arm. It seemed to shake her awake, at least a little bit.

"I think...sometimes there are things we love as kids, and then we forget about them as we grow up, either by accident or because we think we should. And then one day we remember them, and it's like, why did I think I had to give this up? And that's how I feel whenever I go to the fabric store by myself now. I love all of the variation of fabric, patterns, designs; all of it is so...pretty and soothing to me. There are even *sounds* of the fabric store that are comforting to me, like when the workers roll out a bolt of fabric onto the table when they're getting ready to cut it for you? And it's like, *thump, thump, thump.*" She smiled, looking straight at me. "And the scissors when they cut it, they have this very specific snip, you know?"

I did not know. I had no fucking idea what she was talking about. But I was pretty much out of my mind with wanting to kiss her.

But...I didn't.

Because...romantic prowess. Negative three.

And because at that exact moment, a new song started across the room. A song whose opening chords I knew by heart. A song that made me want to twirl Lily back onto the dance floor, hold her close, let her see all of me. But that would have been different from Bonnie Tyler, from Gaga. Even hearing it at all right now felt like a little too much. The stranger who was singing it was killing it. Killing me.

"Are you okay?"

I looked down, and only then realized I must have been spacing out. Lily was biting her lip.

"Sorry," she said. "I'm kind of drunk and didn't mean to...ramble about the fabric store for an hour? Oh my god."

Those splashes of pink returned to her skin and I almost spilled my gin and tonic all over her in my flailing.

"No! No. I could listen to you talk about clothes and the fabric store and your grandma for hours more. Seriously. I just...this song."

Lily tilted her head, listening. "I think I recognize it?"

"It's 'This Charming Man.' By The Smiths."

"Oh." She smiled, just a little, cheeks still pink, almost looking embarrassed. Which...Lily was a rockstar who shouldn't be embarrassed about anything. I had a horrible, sinking feeling that I was fucking this night all up. "The Smiths are definitely too cool for me."

I shook my head vehemently. "No! No, they're really not. Or at least, this song isn't; it's only a pop song, but..." A harsh breath escaped my lips. I suddenly wished I had consumed even a tiny bit less gin.

She had shared her grandma and the fabric store with me. I could share this song with her.

"When I was a teenager, I used to lay on my bed and listen to this song for hours, literally, and feel…"

I trailed off, flailing mentally now. But Lily only looked at me. Eyes patient. Everything about her so fucking soft and strong.

"I don't know. I don't even know what Morrissey was actually singing about in this song, and everything I've learned since then confirms that Morrissey is pretty much an asshole, but when I was a kid and felt…I don't know. Like I was lonely and weird and maybe really fucking gay but maybe not? It was like his voice on this song was the only person who understood. And I really thought that maybe *all* boys sat in their rooms and listened to this song and secretly felt all these things, but it turned out I was…wrong."

I was resting an elbow on the bar now, restlessly drumming fingers against the cold, smudgy counter, unable to meet Lily's eyes and pretty much wanting to die. Lily being excited about the button aisle with her grandma had been a cute anecdote. Me trying to explain "This Charming Man" felt like the equivalent of reaching into my chest and pulling out an album of embarrassing childhood photos that you only engaged when you were really in love with someone and wanted them to see all of your most cringey parts.

But then Lily lifted a hand and trailed her fingers on my wrist, feather light and kind. My fingers stopped drumming.

"It's a beautiful song," she said eventually, her voice almost a whisper.

We were quiet as the performer wrapped up, Lily's fingers still at my wrist, my heart pounding in my ears.

"I don't know if I've ever felt transformed by clothes, like you were talking about," I said eventually, as soon as the song was over. I stared down at the bar, feeling a little shaky, but determined to get the conversation back on track. "It sounds nice. I wish sometimes that I had..." I waved a hand. "More of a fashion sense. If I could express myself better that way. But," I shrugged and looked down at myself, at my black t-shirt and black jeans, "I pretty much only wear this."

She took her hand off mine then. She put her glass, which she had been holding with her other hand, down on the bar. And when I finally looked at her again, her eyes had changed, gone from soft and sympathetic to all sharp and assessing. I quaked a little, in anticipation or self-consciousness or both.

"I think you *do* have a fashion sense, in a way." She smoothed both of her palms over my shoulders, down the sleeves of my shirt. "I love this pocket, first of all. And I associate you with dark colors like these, with that black jean jacket you normally wear. And the fact that I can make any association in my head, of you with clothes, means you *do* have a look. Fashion doesn't have to be fancy."

Her hands traveled down my sides, toward the hem of my shirt, the waistband of my jeans. It was possible I stopped breathing.

She knew my black jean jacket.

She remembered details about me. Like she had noticed me before tonight.

One small thing clicked into place.

"Your jeans could be better, yes," she said, cocking her head, "But honestly, jeans—pants in general—are hard for a lot of bodies, for a lot of reasons, even though we're all conditioned to wear them."

I let out another rough sigh, partly because of the truth

of that, partly because her hands were still resting on my sides.

"I have a hard time figuring out what to wear for work, most of the time," I admitted. "I know I should look like a semi-put together adult, and I don't...know how to do that. Khahkis and dress shirts are kind of a nightmare, and I...don't know what else to do."

"So what *do* you wear to work?"

I looked back down at myself and winced. "Um. A nicer shirt, but pretty much...this?"

"Hmm. Well, first of all, you don't have to wear khakis, Sam. *No one* should have to wear khakis. You simply need to find the *right* pants and shirts, if that's what you want to wear."

She opened her mouth and then snapped it shut.

She picked up her gin and tonic again, chomping rather aggressively on the tiny straw, and stared back toward the dance floor.

I had a feeling she wanted to say something else. And that I knew exactly what it was.

And I didn't feel offended. I felt...suddenly, strangely excited.

"None of your friends have misgendered me all night," I said slowly, trying to figure out how to approach this. It all made sense now. That Lily must have seen my pin. And remembered. Which wasn't actually a small thing at all. "It's been really nice."

"Oh," she said, shrugging. "Of course."

"I've thought about wearing...other things," I said after a beat. "Just to try something different. But I don't know...how to make it not look ridiculous?"

She turned toward me again, one corner of her mouth curved upward.

"What do you mean, ridiculous?"

"I mean," I motioned toward my body. "This is never going to be a Harry Styles situation. I am never going to make that," I pointed to her dress, "look good. And I don't even know if I *want* that. Even though it's beautiful. I..." I frowned. Well, damn. Apparently the magic of Moonie's, and Lily, and too much gin wasn't going to make this any easier. I had been feeling hopeful there for a second.

I leaned back against the bar and let out a breath.

"I only started wearing that they/them pin a year ago," I said, deciding to go all in. I'd already almost cried over Morrissey in front of her, so why the fuck not. "The school's QSA was giving them out. I don't know if I ever would have even contemplated thinking about myself as non-binary, or genderqueer, or whatever I am, if there weren't a ton of my students who identify that way now, and other faculty, too. I thought I would...try it." I scratched at the back of my head. "Fuck, that sounds so dumb. But as soon as I started using they/them, it felt right. Like...I don't know, like what you were talking about when you wear an outfit that actually fits you for the first time?"

Lily smiled. "Yeah."

"I imagine it felt kind of like that. There was just this...*relief* at not having to be a *he*."

She nodded, eyes serious.

"When something really fits," she said carefully, "You suddenly realize how much energy you've been unconsciously devoting to not fitting."

"Yes." I breathed out. "Yes. But...some of my enby students are these like, androgynous supermodels." I kicked at the floor with the toe of my sneaker. "Which, you know, is fine. But even when they're not, they're so fucking confident in who they are. And I feel sometimes like I'm just this imposter, still trying on different outfits to see what works. And maybe, *maybe* this was all part of what I was feeling when I was a kid lying on my bed listening to 'This Charming Man.' And there are just better words for it now. But sometimes I…" I faltered. "I wonder if it would be easier to just take that pin off my jacket. I'm still not good at correcting people who use he/him, because…like, I get it. I'll probably always look like a boring old dude."

Lily shook her head. "Not boring. And not old."

I snorted.

"Lily, I'm in my forties, and all I know is that when I was a kid, it felt like my parents were perpetually in their forties, and that means I'm old. How old are you?"

"Thirty-two."

I gave a dreamy sigh. "Ah. Sweet youth."

She rolled her eyes.

"Anyway. I…" I frowned again. I'd joked, but I actually was a little caught off guard by Lily being over a decade younger than me. Even though I should have guessed this to be true. "I have no idea where I was going with this. I am…drunk."

"You were being honest," she said steadily, "Which I feel honored you trusted me enough with. *And* you were talking about the clothes you wear to work, how they don't feel good. And how you'd look ridiculous if you tried to wear something different. Which is," she huffed, crossing her arms. "Patently untrue. Obviously."

I raised my eyebrows.

"Obviously," I repeated.

"Yes." She squared her shoulders, taking a small step closer to me, as if in challenge. "That's the thing about clothes. It's like…like picking a song to sing at karaoke. You can choose *whatever you want*. And all that matters is that you feel happy when you're singing it. It's nice when the audience sings along with you, but they really don't have to for it to still be powerful, as long as *you* feel it. You know?"

"Okay," I countered. This was what I wanted, working through this with her, but now I was feeling weirdly defensive. I should have expected it. This was how it went when I had asked Claire to help me with makeup, too, a year ago. This sense of possibility, followed by this frustration that I didn't automatically know what to do. That it didn't immediately click. Because when it came to my body, nothing had ever seemed to click. "So what am I going to wear instead? A nice blouse and a pencil skirt?"

Her eyes flared.

"Yes," she said. "If you wanted to."

I guffawed.

"You think I can pull off a *pencil skirt*?"

"Yes," she repeated, again, with feeling.

"Fine," I said, my voice a little too loud. "Tell me what would look good on me, Lily."

Her chest rose and fell. Pink splotches all down her neck.

She took another step closer.

"I think you can wear whatever the hell you want to, Sam Bell," she said, a hand reaching for my hip. "Including this shirt and these jeans for the rest of your life, if they make you happy. But I think a pencil skirt would look nice on you. And...a good V-neck, maybe."

Her hands traveled up to my chest, back to my shoulders. All the air wooshed out of me, the world going topsy turvy, any frustration about dumb gender and my dumb body melting away as the air around us changed. All that mattered were her hands on me, the closeness once again of her body heat, the power of her. All of which made my body feel the opposite of dumb. Like I could absorb some of her Lily-ness through mere proximity. Like the fact that she wanted to touch me at all meant something.

It was the most physical intimacy I'd had in a year. I hoped Scary Bartender was proud of me. I was a little proud of me.

"I would love to see you in a skirt with a snug V-neck sweater. Yeah." Lily nodded, almost as if she were talking to herself. "That would be really fucking hot. There's lots you could do, Sam. I could—"

She stopped suddenly, blanching, and took a step away.

"Sorry. If that was out of line. You can dress however you want, obviously. Sorry."

I opened my mouth to say something. To ask her to go back to that part where I could be *really fucking hot.*

"You don't have to be sorry. I asked."

"I know," she said, face pink again, "but I hate when people give me advice about *my* body, like I haven't already thought about every possible option myself, so. Sorry."

I wanted her fingers on my wrist again. Her palms on my shoulders. Instead, I shoved my hands in my pockets. Considered what to say.

"I don't know if I've thought about every possible option for my body, honestly," I said quietly. And then, "I just still can't believe you think I could fit into a pencil skirt." Like, she had seen my stomach.

Her eyes warmed, like the last embers in a fire sparking back to life.

"I really do," she said sincerely. "Pencil skirts don't have to be confining."

"Well," I said, feeling awkward, but not in a bad way. It had been my choice, to get overly vulnerable with her. And I think I felt...okay. "Thank you."

"You're welcome." And then she actually smiled. She was still so, so close. If she so much as took a deep breath, her breasts—her *great* breasts—would smoosh right into my chest.

She bit her lip.

I got that topsy turvy feeling again.

"I don't care what you wear. But I cannot believe you think you're boring, Professor Bell."

The way her mouth curved, the glint in her eye when she said *Professor Bell*.

Take a deep breath, Lily, I thought.

Instead, Kiki's voice from across the room made her turn her head, take a step away.

"Oh, wow," Lily said. "I can't believe Jonny's actually singing, with Pablo here." A pause. "He must really like him." She turned back to me, a look on her face I couldn't read. "I have to go support him; is that okay?"

"Oh my god, of course." I pushed off from the bar, and it felt like waking up after a dream. "SWV is way more important than this conversation anyway."

"Don't say that." She put a hand on my chest again, for just a moment. I wondered if she could feel my heart beating under her palm. She looked away. "Jonny does slay 'Weak,' though."

He did. And it was sweet, watching Pablo's smile as he watched him, back at their table. It felt safer in general, back at the table in front of the strobe lights of the dance floor. Something had shifted at the bar, and I knew it was my fault. The wanting I could never stop myself from feeling had supercharged when Lily stepped too close to me, when she wasn't just a stranger with a strong voice and a swagger I admired. When she became someone with bittersweet memories, someone who listened to me ramble my nonsense and looked at me with all of her focus. Something had gone downhill when Morrissey came on and my heart, for some reason, decided to bleed all over the floor at her feet, a floor I would never want to look at too closely in the bright light of day.

I didn't know what I was feeling, honestly. If I was ready to go home and forget all of this, or if I had stumbled into something miraculous.

Either way, it was better here, where it was dark and loud and all I had to focus on was my recall of lyrics from songs I used to love. Where the syllables that fell from my mouth needed to be short and sweet, spoken in a shout into the soft shell of Lily's ear, and all she needed to answer with in return was a smile.

4

LILY

WELL, I was fucked.

Sam Bell was supposed to be an experiment for Bold Karaoke Lily, an impulsive decision that would merely add to a fun night out at Moonie's. But even though I had stopped drinking after that last gin & tonic at the bar, I kept getting drunker on Sam anyway, like they were seeping steadily into my bloodstream with each open admission of vulnerability, each shy smile, each horribly belted song.

And I was definitely going to be hungover.

Things got back to karaoke-normal after our stint of oversharing at the bar. My confessions and theirs had made my insides feel all fizzed up, like a bottle of soda dropped on the floor. But back on the dance floor, this night was understandable again. Music, laughter, a bit of lust. Just another night at Moonie's.

Sam and I danced to more songs, from the frenzied hilarity of Reel Big Fish's "Sellout," which was essentially all of us jumping up and down a lot while screaming, to Madonna's "Like a Prayer," which was probably the most animated I'd seen Sam. My friends and I were all dancing in a circle for it, surrounded by the rest of Moonie's—everyone emptied their seats and barstools for "Like a Prayer"—and when the choir part came in, Preeti grabbed Sam's hand and Sam went with it, grabbing her other hand, throwing their head back and lip syncing together, and I felt so deeply happy. It was like the power of Madonna suddenly taught Sam how their hips worked. They looked so relaxed as they twirled and sang along with the rest of us, so far away from the frustration that had momentarily worried their face back at the bar. Under the lights, the blaring speakers, they were just...free. Like an angel sighing.

Their friend Kelsey showed up at one point, slipping into our circle as we danced to Nelly.

"I have friends!" Sam shouted to me excitedly after introducing us.

"I know," I laughed.

Shortly after that, Kelsey sang exactly one song—Michelle Branch's "Everywhere," which brought the house down—and promptly disappeared.

I made Sam sing one more song with me, Dolly's "Jolene," which made them laugh even harder than when I had suggested "Total Eclipse of the Heart." But like the first time, they were a good sport about it, giving it their all, grinning at me over the microphone. Which, by "Jolene," was almost too much for me. No, their scratchy, off-tune voice wasn't made for Dolly—or anything with a melody, maybe—but as I suspected, as they had proven with every other song I ever saw them open their mouth to sing, they knew every single word. Were on beat, line for line. Barely had to glance at the screen for the lyrics. And I had never wanted to fuck anyone harder. When we handed Kiki back our mics, it took everything in me not to grab their hand and stick all of those knobby knuckles into my mouth.

I settled for landing heavily into my chair as we sat back down for a breather, egregiously pressing my thigh into theirs. Their hand reached up and scraped across the back of my neck, brief but burning, making every nerve on my scalp tingle.

"God, you're beautiful," they said, and I wanted to take them then and there. Instead I curled my fingernails into the palm of my hands, dug them in until the pain reminded me that this was temporary, that Moonie's Me was just that. That the more carried away I got, the more I was letting Sam fall for a Lily that wasn't fully real.

It was well past midnight by then, and soon Jonny and Pablo took off, hand in hand. I felt tired but happy, a little loopy, my throat sore from hours of singing. Like always after a night at Moonie's, my voice would be a dry husk for the next twenty-four hours.

It felt like a blink, but soon Kiki was announcing last call, the bar slowly but surely emptying out. I was leaning against Sam, my head on their shoulder, their hand making absentminded circles on my knee. It had just sort of seemed to happen, our bodies drifting closer and closer together throughout the night. My eyes drifted closed, the lights of the dance floor hazy flashes of warmth against my eyelids, and it felt remarkably natural, falling asleep against Sam. The only other people left at our table were Preeti and Bri, and I was sure they were making faces at us, like they'd probably been making faces all night. They were going to give me hell on Monday morning at the clinic.

But right now, the clinic felt so far away. That jerk client, who had yelled at me about bloodwork for his dog, bloodwork that his dog needed, and that I knew he could afford—the ones who couldn't afford it never yelled—

seemed like a distant dream. Everything felt unreal except for my own heart beat, Sam's breath falling lightly onto my forehead, tickling my eyelashes. I wanted to actually fall asleep here, rest right here in this moment forever, and never have to think about what would happen tomorrow, and the day after that, and the day after that.

I didn't, of course. Because the bar was about to close.

And because Kiki was saying my name.

I sat up, pulling away from Sam, blinking and confused.

"...that is, if she's awake enough to close out the night for us," Kiki said into the mic, smirking.

Sam nudged my shoulder, made a shooing motion toward the dance floor with a sleepy, encouraging smile.

When I turned toward the screen, I gulped. When had I even requested this song?

I hazarded a glance at Sam, who was sitting with their chin propped in their palm, that calm smile still on their face, and I remembered. After Sam had told me about their favorite song from when they were a teen, that Smiths song, I had put in *my* favorite syrupy song from my youth. And god, I couldn't even remember the last time I'd heard it, but as soon as the first notes of The Bangles' "Eternal Flame" came on, I understood Sam's stricken look at the bar when they heard Morrissey. Because it took me there immediately, back to my childhood bedroom, lavender walls covered with posters of bands I idolized, listening to this song and wondering if anyone would ever love me.

Little Lily was so misguided about so many things, was so consumed with things she wanted to change. Too big and too small all at once. And almost everything that Little Lily didn't know what to do with, Grown Up Lily now loved. Grown Up Lily now knew all those things were strength.

But no matter how put together grown up me was, my voice still couldn't quite hit that slightly breathy, high, sweet vulnerability of Susanna Hoffs. When I started, my voice was rough around the edges from over-singing, but I made my way, shakily, to the first chorus.

But even then, I sounded a little warbly. Normally when I could get loud, stretch out the strongest lines, I was at my best. But this wasn't even just because my throat was scratchy. This was because this song was too fucking earnest, and I was feeling too many things, and was too strung out to be able to hide any of it.

And through all of it, Sam kept looking at me, like they had been looking at me all night. Gentle and admiring and pure. I felt so grateful for them at that moment, no matter what happened next, for giving me this night. For making me feel like I was the most interesting person in the room. For being such a comforting presence, for gifting me with their honesty, for granting me so many precious, casual touches throughout the night that made my skin heat and my belly burn. I felt strangely bared to them in this nearly empty bar, in the middle of what could have been a very ordinary September night, like they were the only one I had ever wanted to sing for. Like their friends abandoned them on purpose, giving me room to find them.

And when I asked, in the song, *Do you feel my heart beating? Do you understand?* I felt like they did. Like they really, really did.

In the middle of the last chorus, while never breaking eye contact, they stood. They walked around the table, leaned against it. Waited.

Kiki came to me, took the microphone out of my hand.

"Go get 'em, tiger," she said with a wink. Gave me a small shove.

They met me halfway. I only took a few steps, and they were there, green eyes dark and serious, although their mouth was still smiling. They cupped both hands around my face. Rubbed a thumb over my cheek.

I heard a high whistle that I instinctively knew was Bri.

And then Sam closed the gap and kissed me.

5

THE SEPTEMBER NIGHT air was chilly when we stumbled outside, waking me all the way up. We waved goodbye to Preeti and Bri as they stepped into a cab. They had been thinking ahead, had called one ten minutes ago.

I continued to take the Not Thinking Ahead At All path when Lily tugged my hand a second later, led me to the side of the building, and shoved me against the wall. It was hard and a little shocking and the complete opposite of Lily's lips on mine again, which were soft and plump and hot, and the combination made me dizzy.

Until, suddenly, she was gone.

"Sorry." Lily huffed out a breath, hands on her hips. I did my best to not flail wildly and crash into her breasts.

"Sorry," she said again, shaking her head. "I didn't think I'd have to do this, give this preamble before we make out, but...my head's gone a little weird, and I really like you, and I don't want you to suck. So. I just need to make sure you're not secretly grossed out by me, and/or that you don't have a fat girl fetish. Even though you're not skinny, either, but you're not capital-f fat like me; you're just...adorably thick. But I've learned that all shapes and sizes of people can be shitty, so." She took a deep breath. "I just have to be sure."

I froze, slack jawed, stuck between horror that Lily was saying any of these things, and weirdly proud about being called *adorably thick*. While it was clear to me that Lily was confident as hell, I had always felt considerably less so, whether due to a possible tiny smidge of dysphoria or the fact that my body shape seemed to be confined to *shapeless blob*. Which had probably been clear to her when we were discussing pencil skirts.

But Lily thought I was *adorably thick*. Two little words, and I couldn't even explain why I liked them so much. Maybe it was just the fact that they came from her. But suddenly I felt...the closest to sexy I'd ever felt. No matter what happened tonight, I was going to carry that phrase with me for the rest of my fucking life.

"Lily." I tried to gather my thoughts, running a hand through my hair. "I mean it when I say you are genuinely beautiful. But...if it makes you feel any better, or can convince you I don't have a fetish, the last person I dated was a skinny ass dude named Dan. Who was really great at sex stuff but sort of bad at...liking me. And you probably didn't need to know any of that, but I'm not objectifying you. Or, like, I am, but just because...you're pretty and I like you."

Romantic prowess: negative six.

But surprisingly, Lily's shoulders relaxed, her face gentling out, like her defensive shield had retracted.

"What do you mean, he was bad at liking you?"

"Oh, you know." I scratched at the back of my head. "Bad at like...asking about my day or wanting me to ask about his, or like...caring about me?" I shrugged.

"So, he was an asshole."

"That seemed to be my friends' conclusion."

She studied me for a moment.

"Did he ever come to karaoke with you?"

"Once, yeah. Why?"

"I'm just picturing myself retroactively booing him."

I huffed out a small laugh. "Well, he didn't sing, so."

"Of course he didn't. Even easier to boo at him, then."

I shuffled my feet, beginning to regret bringing up Dan.

I knew he probably was an asshole. No, he was definitely an asshole. But in bed, no one had ever made me feel so attended to, so...thoroughly debauched, in such an exhilarating way. It seemed hard to believe that someone who treated my body with such care, who made me feel so *good*, physically, couldn't care about me even a little, emotionally. Nate told me this was naive. But that only made me feel even shittier, so I stopped talking about Dan to Nate, or to any of my friends really, after that.

"You know," Lily cocked her head, "I've always been worried that I'm only okay at sex stuff. Like, how do you *know*, really?"

This shocked a laugh out of me.

"Me too. Although, well." I scratched needlessly at my hair again, face flushing. "Dan did teach me some stuff."

"Wow," Lily breathed. "I really hate Dan."

I smiled at her. The night was still cold, but warmth was sliding back into my blood.

"I would really like it if we stopped talking about Dan now. Do you believe me? That I want you?"

"Oh, yeah. I'm sorry. I knew you did. I just...got freaked out. Sorry. Although…"

"Yeah?"

"It was really cute watching you squirm."

She grabbed my shirt and pulled me back to her.

"I would very much like to have mediocre sex with you, Sam," she whispered into my lips, which made me laugh, so it took my brain a second to catch up with the fact that finally, she was kissing me again, and her tongue gliding past my lips was just as sweet as I'd imagined.

I fell back against the wall and she came with me, parting my legs with her thigh, her hands weaving into my hair, fingernails scratching at my scalp. A noise escaped my throat, raw from karaoke, and she growled back, pressing her body into mine. And everything about it felt right, comfortable and satisfying: transformative. The perfect fit.

GOD, I loved kissing this adorable nerd.

It was embarrassing, that I'd shown my insecurities in asking those questions—I shouldn't have to do that shit anymore, and it had been obvious all night that Sam liked me. Was attracted to me. But when the door of Moonie's shut behind us and we were out in the cool, quiet night, away from the contained safety of the bar, I got scared. I wasn't ready for Bold Lily to disintegrate, for this bubble to burst. And I was still a little fucked up from "Eternal Flame." So, yes, I was freaking out.

But then Sam had called me pretty.

Do you believe me? That I want you?

People had used *beautiful* with me, plenty of times, until it almost became this conciliatory, meaningless thing, this unnecessary reassurance that fat can be beautiful. Like a sunset is beautiful, or a Christmas tree, or a rainbow. Generic and safe. A different kind of safe than Moonie's safe: safe as a means of hiding messier truths.

Somehow, though, *pretty* sent shivers down my spine. *Pretty* felt specific to my skin.

And *want* reflected everything filling up my gut, using the strength of my body to push Sam up against this wall outside of Moonie's. I never wanted to back away from this wall, because I feared that once I did, once we stepped into a car and drove away from this place, the spell would be broken. I would go back to quiet, ordinary Lily. But here, with Sam's tongue in my mouth and their hands on my body, I was made of want. And I felt like a queen.

And so I made my decision. As long as Sam's body was touching mine, it would be like the magic of Moonie's was still watching over us. I could still be the person Sam thought I was, for a bit longer, until the dawn broke.

And I would make it worth my while.

I tore my lips away to pull in a few ragged breaths. The light from the huge white sign out front, shouting *The Moonlight Café* into the middle of nowhere, as if you could miss it—the only other things out here were train tracks and dusty excavators—cast a pale glow on Sam's face. Their eyes looked dark, heavy lidded. My bright red lipstick was smudged all over their mouth. I didn't have the kind of excess cash on my receptionist salary for high quality lipstick, but at the moment, I was grateful for it. It made Sam look sexy as fuck. Heat pooled between my legs, between my lungs, in the pulse of my fingertips, and I desperately wanted Sam to feel as sexy as they had made me feel all night. But I wanted to do it right.

"Honest question," I said, brushing a curl off their forehead. "If I am thinking really filthy thoughts about your body—say, your dick in particular—is that a form of misgendering you? Because I'll stop if so."

Sam closed their eyes for a moment, a shudder passing over their shoulders.

"It's...complicated," they said. "For other people, yes. Probably. I don't know. For me, almost all of my fucked up feelings about gender are…" they waved their hand in circles in front of their face, and then their chest. Their heart. "Here."

And then, almost a whisper: "I want to turn you on. My body is yours, Lily."

I put a hand there, over their heart. Felt its strong, steady rhythm.

And then I put my other hand between their thighs, over the bulge in their jeans, and I gave a small squeeze.

Sam made a sound that sounded something like, "Mmmnergh," and dropped their forehead to my shoulder.

"Can I ask," they spoke into my neck, their hot breath on the exposed skin there warranting them another squeeze from my hand, "what filthy thoughts you were having about, uh…me?"

"Oh, mainly that I need you inside of me, like, *right now.*"

My hand slid up, fingertips skirting their soft belly. Tried to slip my hand down between their jeans and their briefs, but it was too tight. Dammit, Sam, you deserved better jeans. I went for the button and zipper instead, my other hand falling down to help.

"Lily," Sam breathed. "If you go much further, I'm going to fuck you against the wall of Moonie's."

"And?"

"And I really don't want to do that. It's probably very dirty, for one thing, and your clothes are very pretty."

Oh. Well. They had a point there.

"Then call a fucking car, Sam," I huffed out. And with a shaky laugh, they pulled their phone out of their back pocket, and they did.

"My place okay?" they asked.

"Yes." My place was an absolute mess at the moment,

which I hated, and I didn't want Sam to see it. I bet their place would be nice and neat, full of interesting artifacts from around the world, whatever kinds of things history professors collected.

Professor Bell. I remembered the way their pupils had widened, back at the bar, when I'd called them that. I made a mental note to make plentiful use of the phrase over the next few hours.

When the car was requested, Sam stuck the phone back in their pocket, mumbling, "Ten minutes," before reaching their hands around my backside and pulling me fully back to them. Their mouth went to my neck this time, sucking on my earlobe a bit, which had always been my very favorite thing, and I let myself make a purring noise as I ran my fingers through their hair. I couldn't believe I had been nearly asleep twenty minutes ago. Every corner of me buzzed alive now, and Sam was exploring every one of those corners of me, with their mouth, with their hands over the thin fabric of my dress. And fuck, I spent two weeks getting this dress right, but how I wanted to rip it off right now so that those hands could make contact with all of my skin.

I could count the people I'd been physically intimate with on one hand, but even of those, there had been at least two who seemed happy to kiss my mouth but were strangely hesitant to touch my body. As if touching my fat rolls would unpleasantly highlight their existence. But none of my rolls or my curves or my dimples seemed to present a roadblock to Sam's hands, and by the time our car pulled up, I was panting and aching for them.

"Fuck," I said when Sam stepped back. "This is going to be the best hookup ever."

Sam froze. They were still only a foot away from me, so I saw the confused look on their face, the way their eyes clouded over, a crease forming in their brow. It was only a second, and then they seemed to shake it off. "Yeah," they said, distractedly, and turned around to walk to the car. My heart sank.

I didn't know why I'd said it. I was turned on beyond reason and wasn't thinking clearly. It sounded silly and flippant, and I hoped Sam knew I didn't feel flippant about any of this.

But maybe it was good that I said it.

Because we had only truly known each other for a few hours. And most of those hours had been spent dancing and singing. We barely knew each other, and now we were going to go fuck each other's brains out. It seemed pretty clear. Sam had to know this had all the markings of a one-night stand, right?

Of course, I'd never actually had a one-night stand before. But it seemed like a practice Bold Lily would be able to handle.

And a one-night stand could still be meaningful. Right?

God, I didn't want to hurt Sam.

I tried to take deep gulps of air before I opened the car door and stepped in. But even then, I had to work on not making my labored breathing overly obvious to the Lyft driver as the wheels of her car crunched over the gravel parking lot, before it pulled onto the bypass and left Moonie's behind. Sam and I sat silently on either side of the backseat, and even though they were right there, their absence made my heart flutter, a little pulse of panic. I hated the awkwardness I had just injected into the air between us, and the real world crept in with each rotation of the car's tires.

Touching, we had to be touching. That was what I had promised myself.

Stay in the moment. Hold on to the night. Sam was an

adult; they knew what they were getting into. This could still be magic.

I reached my hand over, leaned in a bit, rested my palm on the inside of Sam's thigh. Their leg dropped open immediately for me, and I smiled, the ache in my chest loosening as my hand moved slowly upward. Until Sam hissed out a "Lily" in whispered warning, and I stopped. Instead, I coached their arm to rest on the seat between us, palm up.

And until the car stopped at Sam's apartment many minutes later, I ran my fingers in small circles along that palm, around their wrist, up their forearm and back, listening closely for how their breath hitched, feeling the slightest shivers tremor beneath their skin, feeling more like Bold Lily than I had ever felt. It was even better than the power of Carrie or Dolly, feeling the goosebumps rise along Sam's arms. Knowing that I was the one who had put them there.

6

SAM

I DROPPED my keys on the ground. Kicked the front door shut. And pushed Lily against the wall, Lily with her feather-light fingers that had made me so hard in the Lyft I could barely think straight. And I was feeling pretty good about myself, honestly—that was some damn good romantic prowess, the door kicking and everything—and thought Lily felt the same, being that she took my lower lip between her teeth and *tugged*, but a second later, she leaned away with a frustrated groan.

"Listen, I love the urgency, I really do, but we already did the wall thing at Moonie's and my feet are killing me. I need a bed, like, pronto."

I nodded. "Done and done."

As I led her into my bedroom, I was grateful my tiny apartment was relatively clean, that I had wasted away this afternoon until I could leave for Moonie's doing the dishes and going through my stacks of junk mail and sorting through the clothes I inevitably left in a pile on my floor each week, to later be separated into "should wash" and "eh, could wear again."

Not that Lily seemed to be paying much attention to my apartment.

She slipped her velvet jacket off her shoulders as soon as we entered the bedroom, and looked like she was moving to take off her dress, too, until I quickly interfered.

"Wait." I walked behind her to the zipper. "Can I?"

"Fine," she huffed, that same frustration in her voice as she'd had outside of Moonie's. It drove me wild. "But don't be all slow about it. I'm dying here."

I grinned, nestling my nose between her shoulder blades, the curves of her back, as the dress slid off her hips, as I got to work on her bra. She released a heavy, happy sigh when I worked it off her shoulders, mumbling "goddamn devil underwires" as it fell to the floor. I slid to my knees, lips skating down her spine until they reached her underwear, all the while trying to breathe her in, take the heat of her skin into my own, squeeze this moment for all it was worth.

Because, as she had reminded me back at Moonie's, this was a hookup.

Which...was one of those words I had always found to be a little nebulous, honestly.

Maybe I could have asked Lily for more details about what she meant, but I felt, instinctually, from the way she had said it, that I wouldn't like the answer. That I already knew it. That the tiny voice of reason in my head was dancing on some squishy piece of gray matter somewhere, shouting, *Told you so*.

And that if I had asked, it might have ruined whatever happened next. And now that we had gotten to that *next* part—I loved the shake of Lily's hips as she helped me wiggle her underwear down her legs—I was so very glad to be here.

Even though every fiber of my being felt like this was the farthest thing from a *hookup* I could imagine.

I smoothed my hands over those hips, down those wonderful thighs, intent on blocking the word *hookup* from my brain and focusing on the moment. Which I did by planting an open mouthed kiss over Lily's left butt cheek, pressing my tongue into the dimples.

"Sam," she said after a minute, her voice raspy, "Come on. I want to see you."

Fair enough. But I gave her butt a good bite, for good measure, smiling at her hiss before I stood back up and twirled her around. She smacked my shoulder, eyes full of fire.

"You are...*ugh*." And then she was kissing me, hard and ruthless, her hands yanking at the waistband of my jeans. "Just—fucking—get them off," she said into my lips, and I was pretty sure her voice was all hoarse like that mostly because of karaoke, but there was also lust in there, for *me*, which was completely illogical but I'd take it.

The lust dropped away a bit, though, a second later, when she leapt away from me and screamed.

I had my pants halfway down my legs and almost fell straight on my face.

"Oh my god," Lily wheezed, "It's just," wheeze, "a fucking cat. Sorry." Her hand was still clutching at her chest. "It," wheeze, "startled me."

I looked down. And watched Garfunkel lovingly twining his way in and out of Lily's legs, purring against her ankles.

"Goddammit, Garfunkel." I yanked my jeans back up and quickly scooped him into my arms, tossing him unceremoniously into the living room. "Where is Simon," I muttered to myself, looking around until I saw him staring at me from the top of the fridge. Obviously.

"You monsters behave yourselves," I said before slamming the bedroom door shut.

I turned back to Lily, desperately hoping my cats had not ruined the moment, because if they had, I swear to fucking—

"Strip," Lily said, arms crossed over her chest. There was an amused look on her face, but that raspy voice was serious.

Alrighty then.

I yanked my pants off, and my underwear, and then my shirt, and hopped around for a second getting my socks off, because there was nothing more humiliating than being naked except for socks, and I was sure it was all very undignified but Lily seemed satisfied by it. Because when I stood back up, fully naked, she said, "*Finally*," and pointed to the bed. "Go."

And holy shit, I liked being bossed around by Lily. It was like every fantasy I'd ever mildly contemplated while watching her sing "Before He Cheats," but a million times better. Because I also knew how soft she was now. How patches of pink bloomed on her neck and her chest when she thought she had said too much. How fragile she looked when she sang that last song in an almost empty Moonie's, how I had wanted to sink to the floor with her, wrap her in my arms and never let her go.

I scrambled under the sheets and she came with, and I jumped on top of her with a level of glee I knew my body would pay for later. I had gotten the picture by this point that she was impatient, so I tried to be quick with exploring her body with my mouth, making my way down to her thighs, but damn, I wanted to be more thorough. Maybe she'd let me be more thorough later.

I had only ever been with a couple of women before, and both had been a long ass time ago—and one had turned out to be a lesbian—so I felt a little nervous as I settled in between Lily's thighs, hands tracing up the tender skin there. I wanted to be good at this for Lily. Because I didn't actually want to have mediocre sex with Lily. I wanted to blow her mind.

"Professor Bell," she rasped, and it was like those two words by themselves somehow forced pre-cum to ooze out of my cock. Fucking A, I was *really* never going to let any student ever call me that again. "I don't know what you're staring at down there, because I've seen it and it's honestly not that exciting, but if you don't put your mouth on me soon I'm going to lose my mind. Just as an FYI."

I laughed, and it loosened my nerves.

I opened her up with my fingers, and she was so wet, so slick on my fingers and my tongue, that it gave me all the confidence I could ever need, and it was easy. So easy to lick her where she needed to be licked, to hum my pleasure against her clit when she voiced hers. I loved how she tasted, the intimacy of oral, how it brought you to the earthy, carnal realness of sex, the weird wonderfulness of our bodies. That our pleasure centers were these odd fucking aliens but there were so many ways to make them feel good, so many ways we could make each other feel good, no matter what kind of body we had. Which was why I increasingly hated the entire concept of gender the more I let myself think about it.

We were all just aliens. We all fit together.

There were probably so many ways to fit together that we hadn't even thought of yet.

"Sam." Lily's voice was oddly high pitched, and it made me pull away in alarm.

"You okay?"

I had been sort of involved in my clit-labia-alien world down there for a while, and I blinked up at her, taking in that her chest was rising and falling in heavy gusts, that her forehead was damp. She grinned at me, eyes sparkling, and I tried, for about the fortieth time in her presence tonight, to not combust.

"Yes. But come here." She motioned limply with a hand and I followed, my knees aching as I readjusted, locking my elbows at her sides. "Just give me a second." She ran her hands over my shoulders, down my chest. "I'm not good at multiple orgasms. I don't want to come yet. Want to come with you, when you're inside of me."

This sounded hot and vulnerable all at once, and I rested my forehead on hers, taking in some needed breaths of my own.

"Okay," I said. "We can make that happen. Just tell me when you're ready."

Her hands kept traveling over my chest, my stomach. I tried not to wince. Even though I loved how it felt.

"You don't like your body," she said, so softly, and I wanted to die a little. Although, as if to soften the blow, she reached down and gently cupped my balls, and honestly, it helped. "Is it dysphoria or something else?"

"I don't know," I said, honestly. I opened my mouth again to say more, to say that I mainly just thought my body wasn't all that attractive, but then I closed it again. Because maybe dysphoria did play a small part. Maybe it always had and I just didn't know. Which felt...I don't know. Embarrassing. But maybe it shouldn't be. Maybe it was okay. "I don't know," I repeated.

She nodded. Brought her hands and her eyes back up to my face. Her hair knots were ever so slightly akimbo now, her cheeks flushed, eyes soft.

"Well. I think you're gorgeous, Sam Bell," she whispered, and something inside me felt like it cracked. A touch of pain, but more openness left in its wake.

"I'm ready," she said after a steady minute of me staring at her, once again not knowing what to say. "God, Sam." She touched my hair. "I am so ready for you to fuck me."

And so I did. It was like I was barely conscious for the putting on of the condom, for the rearranging of limbs, but when I slid into her, still so slick and tight and *present*, I was aware of everything. How incredible it felt. The way Lily's mouth dropped open, the way her eyes almost closed but didn't, keeping a hazy watch on me the whole time as I thrust into her, how it made me feel like a god. Or a goddess. Or some ephemeral genderless being full of heat and light. How the thickness of her thighs caged around me made me feel so fucking safe and close to her. How our skin felt, sliding against each other, the softness and friction of it.

"Sam," she said, when I could feel she was close, when I was starting to lose my own grip on things, "Talk to me."

The words fell out of me, nonsensical and ridiculous, and I realized as my own orgasm started to claw its ways into my toes that I wasn't even sure who I was talking to, her or me or both of us at once, that we were both beautiful and hot and good, and the cry she made when she came, her eyes finally squeezing shut, was the best sound I had ever fucking heard. It sent me tumbling over the edge seconds later. It felt endless, this tight spiral of bliss, like our bodies were infinity, like we were born to feel only this.

But of course, we weren't infinity; we were mortal little aliens, and I collapsed onto my elbows as I came down, breathing heavily into Lily's collarbone.

"Fuck," I said.

"Same," she replied. She made little circles with her fingertips on my back, and I closed my eyes, skin tingling everywhere, drinking it in. Until finally, regretfully, I had to pull out, and creakily make my way to the bathroom. When I got back, Lily was already half asleep.

"I should go pee," she mumbled as I wrapped my comforter around us. "But. Mmm. Tired."

I kissed her temple. "You do you, Lily." Even though she was right. She should definitely pee. But she only smiled, eyes closed, and blindly threw an arm around me.

Within minutes, she was asleep.

7

LILY & SAM

HOURS LATER, I woke to weak light filtering through the sole window in Sam's bedroom. It was still early, far too early to be awake on a day after karaoke. My head ached; my throat was a desert. Maybe it was the unease of being in a different bed that awoke me; maybe Sam had shifted in their sleep and surprised my system.

I looked over at them, resting next to me, and they looked so peaceful. Their hair was delightfully tousled, the whiskers on their chin that had scratched my skin last night more defined. We had drifted in the night, but one of their ankles was still hooked around mine. It was hard to look at them, their loveliness yanking on my gut like an anchor, making me doubt everything: what we had done last night, what I was going to do next. Making me want to stay.

So I looked at the walls instead. I had barely comprehended anything about Sam's apartment last night, other than it was small and neat and had lots of nicely framed things on the walls. But now, in the dim light, the lust drained from my system—not completely, with the heat of their body still so close to mine, the preciousness of their

sleeping face, but enough that I could think more clearly—
I realized I was completely surrounded by maps.

Straight ahead, the wall opposite the bed seemed dedi-
cated to maps of subway systems: mazes of angular,
brightly colored lines and interlocking zig zags. London.
Tokyo. Boston. Paris. New York. Seoul.

To my left, next to the window, there was a large map
of National Parks of the United States.

I craned my head, tried to see what was above Sam's
headboard. Something sepia toned and historical looking,
a spider's web of patterns and boundaries and landmarks.

Finally, I took a deep breath and looked at Sam again.
They were so quiet, the in and out of their breathing the
most soothing, gentle thing. I wanted to meditate to it, let it
work itself into all of my sore spots.

Instead, I leaned over and pushed their shoulder.

Later, I would wonder why I did it. Why I didn't just
get up, quietly gather my things, and leave.

At the time, something about it made sense in my
head. The dawn might have been breaking, but we were
still touching, technically. And they had asked me something about myself, back at the bar at Moonie's, when we'd
talked about clothes. Something that made me happy. I'd
never had a chance to ask them something back, about
what brought *them* joy. I needed to finish the circle, before I
untangled my ankle from theirs. Before the night was officially over.

"Hey," I whispered, shaking them again. Their eyes
blinked open, and they lifted their head, looking confused.
They stared at me for a second, the blurriness in their eyes
clearing just a bit, before they smiled and dropped their
head back to the pillow.

"Hey," they said. And ugh, that satisfied, half asleep
smile. Kill me. "You okay?"

"Tell me why you love history," I said. "And subway systems maybe."

"What?" They laughed, but it wasn't their weird snorting laugh. It was more like an amused breath.

I nodded to the maps surrounding us.

"History. Why do you teach it?"

They blinked a few more times. And then they rubbed a hand over their face.

"Um," they said. "This isn't quite the postcoital conversation I'm used to? Not that I'm really used to post-coital anything, these days."

"I want to know," I insisted. "Just tell me one thing."

I think...I was searching for a souvenir. One thing I could take with me. Something that would always make me remember Sam Bell.

They looked at me for a long moment, brow slightly furrowed. And I knew whatever they ended up saying, the souvenir was always going to be this. The way they looked at me. From the corner of a dark room. While they were inside me. Half awake in a dimly lit room, their eyes sleepy and thoughtful.

Taking me seriously, every single time.

"Well, as for subway systems, they are incredible," they said matter-of-factly. "We built trains? *Underground?* What, and I cannot stress this enough, *the fuck?*"

I laughed. Which was the worst. If they kept making me laugh, I'd probably end up crying.

"And subway *maps* are the best, obviously," they said.

"Obviously."

"Look at them!" They waved a hand. "All the patterns and different colors. So satisfying. I feel like that's something you understand, yeah?"

They looked at me, eyes bright, and I nodded. I understood it so well.

It felt like they were inside me again, but in a different way, a way that made me ache even more.

They turned their face toward the ceiling.

"As for history…" They went quiet, their face serious. "It makes me feel calm. The fact that we can collect these little pieces of the past, and put them together in a way that makes sense. In a way that sounds logical. Because so much of what happens in modern day, current life feels so messy, so awful. It never makes sense, as we're living it. It makes me feel better to know that someday, years from now, some nerdy historian will collect pieces from this moment and write a paper that says, *This is what happened at this moment in time, and this is why it happened. This is what we've learned from it.* Even if what that ends up being is that we fucked everything up, I have to believe some person out there in the future will be able to talk about it really eloquently, at least. And be like, wow, those Americans were dumb. Let's examine all the ways the American experiment went wrong from the start, in neat bullet points and timelines that everyone can clearly understand."

They paused. Another laugh-breath.

"It is maybe weird that that thought soothes me."

"It's not weird at all," I said. Or, more accurately, croaked. I desperately needed a glass of water. "I wish I could watch you teach."

"Oh, god. You really don't." They turned back toward me and shrugged their shoulder that was now facing the ceiling, the tiniest bit of color creeping into their cheeks. "I don't know if I'm any good at it, but it's where I've ended up. Sometimes, though…" They drifted off, and I nudged them again.

"What?" I grinned. "Say it. I want to hear you compliment yourself."

They laughed, and it was almost a snort. The color in their cheeks darkened.

"Sometimes—not as often as I should, probably, but still sometimes—I actually get to see a kid have a break-through. Of like, fuck, this is all so much more complicated than what I thought I knew. And that realization is like...*it*, you know? That's all history is. Knowing that you know nothing, but being stubborn enough to still want to try to learn *something*, if you can."

I hoped I always remembered the way their eyes looked right then, so very green and smart and sexy and good.

"Did any of that make any kind of sense? I'm still half-asleep here."

"It did," I whispered. "Thank you for telling me all that, Professor Bell."

Their mouth curved, a soft crescent.

"And I like maps in general because I'm a nerd. I've always wanted to travel the world, but I'll never be able to. So I like to make believe."

"What do you mean you'll never be able to?"

"Because I wracked up a ton of student debt and then ended up in a job that doesn't make a ton of money." Another shrug. "It's okay; it's my choice. I could choose another, better paying job if I wanted to. And I've tried. It just turned out that I was really bad at everything else. So...I collect maps instead, and daydream. And milk my memories of that one semester I did in Rome over twenty years ago. And watch a lot of YouTube. It's almost as good as plane tickets. God, I am talking a *lot* for barely being awake. Do you want coffee or something? Or should we be making out? I can definitely brush my teeth if you're up for that. I'm up for that. For the record."

I snuggled further into the pillow. I found myself dangerously close to wanting to know everything. About the other jobs they'd had. About their semester in Rome. About all the places they wanted to go. I would listen to it all.

I also *was* up for making out. But no.

The night was almost over.

The sun was creeping higher into the sky. Real life Lily had things to do today, to prepare for the work week.

So instead I asked the most innocuous of all the questions in my brain.

"What do you watch on YouTube?"

"You seriously want to know?"

And even though their voice was incredulous, the look on their face was so eager. Like I had asked the right question. It was adorable, and my heart almost cracked in two.

"Yes," I whispered.

"Well, in that case." They grinned. "Lily. I watch *so much*."

I REACHED over the side of the bed to grab my phone from the pocket of my jeans.

"There are a million travel vlogs, obviously," I said, clicking on the red and white app. "And seriously, the museums of the world are doing *amazing* work on the Internet these days. But," I clicked through my subscription list, "what I've been really into lately? Are the trains."

"The trains," Lily repeated, a hint of a smile in her voice. I looked over at her, just to double check that I wasn't going too hardcore nerd here, that the tone of her voice was affectionate and not a thin veil for oh-my-god-shut-up-and-let-me-fall-back-asleep. Which I wouldn't be opposed to either, honestly. I had no idea what time it was, but I was exhausted.

But even through my dazed semi-consciousness, I was a bit exhilarated from talking about my life with Lily at Whatever Unknown Hour of the Morning. It felt a bit like when I was a mere youth in college, and would spit out my best papers at 3am. Or maybe the papers actually weren't that great, but I definitely had some *great* conversations at 3am with my friends.

Actually, scratch that; I bet the conversations were probably the worst, too.

But they *felt* like the best, and that's what talking to Lily right now felt like. Like maybe I actually *had* gotten the answers to her questions right. The way she looked at me, slightly entertained but her eyes all twinkly, too, made me feel like something was going right. The fact that she had even woken me up to ask me such questions was—well, kind of weird, but also kind of sweet.

And the fact that she snuggled onto my shoulder when I brought up the first train video instead of raising a skeptical eyebrow—could've gone either way, in my estimation —felt like something was definitely going right.

After we watched a few minutes of train footage, I'd move the conversation back to her. Ask her more about her job, how long she'd worked there, if she wanted to keep making clothes as a hobby or if she'd ever thought about doing it professionally. Kort ran her own small business, pounding copper in a rather violent fashion into surprisingly delicate jewelry; maybe she could give Lily some advice.

Or maybe we shouldn't talk about work at all; maybe we should just get breakfast and talk about our favorite breakfast foods. Or I could make us tea to soothe our throats and then we could have lots more sex.

"This guy's in Serbia a lot," I said into her hair as the video started. "There's no commentary, just the countryside going by. For hours. So it really feels like you're there. It's weird, but whenever I'm feeling anxious, a train video always calms me down."

Lily hummed into my chest.

It was the last thing I remembered.

The next time I woke up, the sun was higher in the sky, harsher against my eyelids. My phone was facedown on my chest.

And I must have been wrong.

Things must not have been going right after all.

Because Lily was gone.

8

—————

SAM

FOR THE SMALLEST MOMENT, a lick of hope flared in my chest when I picked the phone up and saw the notifications for new texts. Before my bleary eyes comprehended that they were from Claire and Kort.

I realized then that I had never actually gotten Lily's number. Hadn't even thought about it.

I didn't even know her last name.

Romantic prowess: negative five hundred.

I closed my eyes, took a few breaths in and out before I stood—damn, I was sore—and did a cursory sweep of the apartment.

But as suspected, Lily had not left a note.

Claire: *omg Sam! Is it true nobody showed to karaoke?? But you always get there so early; don't tell us you were there alone :(*
Kort: *SERIOUSLY SAM IF THIS HAPPENED I WILL DIE*
Claire: *text us back ASAP to tell us what happened & tell us you don't hate us*

Kort: *but I mean if you did I would understand, personally*

I threw my phone on my dresser and flopped back onto the bed.

I allowed myself twenty minutes to curl into the tiniest ball I could. Squeeze my eyes shut. Breathe in the scents barely still present on my pillows—citrus perfume and sex —and feel what I wanted to feel: complete devastation.

My brain was a torpedo of Lily: her voice slicing me wide open. Her hips swinging as she sunk herself low, low, low on the dance floor. The ghost of her thighs pressed tight against mine, warm skin against warm skin. Her hands curving over my shoulders, my chest, my hips when we were at the bar, telling me I could look sexy. The echo of her laugh, tingling in my ear, sinking down to my toes. The comfort of waking up next to her, ankle hooked around mine, mouth full of questions. Wanting to know me. Making me feel like I was interesting and worthwhile.

She had come to me, back at Moonie's. She. Had come. To me.

I curled myself inward. Clenched my fists. Let the sadness flow over me like a wave.

And then I took a deep, ragged breath. I drank a full glass of water and took three ibuprofen. I fed Simon and Garfunkel. I brushed my teeth.

I steeled myself for the day, and for tomorrow, and the day after that.

I wasn't going to be dramatic about this. I was not.

And I wasn't, for a while. Because, well. I fell back asleep.

And was only woken up hours later by a loud, jolting pounding on my door.

I would have ignored it if I could, but I had this neighbor Agnes who was older and got confused sometimes. She definitely shouldn't be living by herself, but I didn't know what to do about it, other than open the door when she knocked and answer her questions about the weather report, and assure her that the truck that backfired last night in the street had *not* been a gunshot, and listen to her talk about Jackie Onassis sometimes.

Anyway, it wasn't Agnes.

"What are you doing here?"

"Nice to see you too, friend." Kort pushed past me into my apartment, and I couldn't even block her because she was carrying a small human on her chest.

"Have you been checking your phone? We were worried."

I closed the door behind Claire, who was my oldest friend. Who was going to make me talk about my feelings. Fuck.

"Uh. No. Hold on."

I escaped to my bedroom and picked up my phone.

Claire: *Sam, can you respond?? I want to make sure you're not dead*

Kort: *no, she's just feeling guilty and thinks you hate us*

Kort: *but I hope you're not dead, too, for the record*

Claire: *also Harry stopped vomiting and Kort really wants to get out of the house*

Kort: *a legitimate cause for celebration*

Claire: *Can we come over? I feel like we haven't hung out in a long time and I really am sad about missing last night : (*

Kort: *okay bitch, you never responded so now claire actually thinks you hate her, good job*

Kort: *we are coming over to make sure you're not dead*

When I walked back into the living room, Kort was

bouncing Harry on her chest, and Claire was sitting at the edge of my favorite chair, frowning.

"So are you okay? You look super tired."

I flopped onto the couch. "A night at Moonie's does that to you. You know that."

Both Claire and Kort's eyes went wide. In like, the exact same way. Lesbians.

"So you *did* go?" Claire asked.

"Oh my god," Kort grinned, "Did you really go and sit by yourself in a corner for like five hours? Because I can totally see you doing that, actually. This is kind of amazing."

"No, I did not sit by myself in a corner," I said sharply. At least, not for *hours*.

"So what happened?" Claire asked.

I draped an arm over my eyes. Tried to hold in a dramatic sigh.

"Okay. So you know that other big group that's there a lot, that sits at the table right next to the dance floor?"

"Of course." I could picture Claire's nod, the trying-to-understand look of concern on her face. "They seem like good people."

"Oh, and there's that woman in their group you have a crush on," Kort said, almost casually. I raised my arm to stare at her in dismay.

"How do you know that?"

"Come on, Sam. You're always spellbound when she sings. And there was also the fact that the last time we were at Moonie's, at the end of the night when you were really drunk, you kept talking about how you wanted her to step on your face. Or something. I don't remember the exact phrasing, but it was entertaining."

"Oh." I stared at the ceiling. "I do not remember that." And then, covering my face again: "Iamsuchanidiot."

"Waaaait a second." And now I could picture the look on *Kort's* face: predatory. Gleeful. "Sam. What. Happened. Last. Night."

I thought I knew, I thought.

But right now, in the cold, hungover light of day, I felt at a loss.

"Well. The, uh, woman who I wanted to step on my face invited me to sit at their table, so...I hung out with their group all night."

"She invited you to sit at their table?" Claire repeated.

"It was fun," I said weakly. It had been. I was relatively confident on that point.

"Hold up," Kort said. "Are you telling us you made new friends?"

"Aw!" I could picture Claire's eyes lighting up. "Sam, you made new friends!"

"I don't like it." I moved my arm to see Kort shaking her head. "You're not allowed to make new friends. Only us."

"You're the ones who abandoned me!"

"*Vomit.*" Kort said. "*Projectile.*"

"Your choice to reproduce."

Kort opened her mouth. Then nodded and resumed bouncing. "Yeah. That's fair."

"So is that the only reason why you haven't been answering your phone?" Claire pushed. "Because you stayed out late at Moonie's and were hungover?"

I *could* have said yes. But I was bad at lying. And it was Claire.

I covered my face with both arms this time.

"Fine. Lily—the one who invited me to their table— and I kind of...clicked. I thought we clicked really well, actually. So we sort of slept together?"

Claire gasped and hit my side. Kort let out a low whistle.

"This," Kort said, "is incredible. I can*not* believe we all missed this."

"Kelsey did show up at one point," I remembered. "I was pretty drunk. Don't know if I introduced her to Lily or not. She sang one song and left."

Kort laughed. "Of course she did."

"Sam," Claire gushed, "I'm so excited for you! This is the first person you've slept with since Dan, right? And she doesn't even seem like a gigantic asshole, from what I can remember of her, anyway. Personal growth, Sam!"

"Yeah, well."

God, I wished Claire hadn't mentioned Dan. Because everything I was feeling felt remarkably, horribly Dan-ish.

Like I had thought something special had happened to me—that the wanting between us had been the same—and then I woke up and discovered I must have had it all wrong from the start.

It was hard not to feel like last night had been the nail in the coffin. How many times could I do this to myself?

Even though it had truly felt like it was different. But wasn't that how it always felt, at the start of something? Maybe it was merciful, to have whatever existed between Lily and me not even get past the beginning.

Back to the plan, then. Fully commit myself to a life of Crushes Only. A future of eternal pining. Fantasies that could never hurt me.

I really didn't think it would be that bad.

After I got over Lily.

Or more accurately, after I got over the possibility of her.

"Yeah, well, *what?* Good god, Sam, lower your arms.

You look like a pouting teenager." Claire yanked on an arm and I let it fall away. "What happened?"

"She...left."

"So text her," Kort said. "Tell her you want to hang out again. You deserve someone good, Sam."

Oh no, Kort was being nice to me. I must have seriously looked rough.

"I...didn't get her number? Anyway," I waved a hand, "She made it pretty clear that it was just...you know." I couldn't bring myself to say the word. A *hookup.*

"Nevermind," Claire said. "I take it back. She *is* a gigantic asshole."

"No," I said immediately. "No. She's not. She's...*blergh.*" I blew out a breath.

"Oh, Sam," Claire said softly. "You really like her."

"Of course I do," I said. And horrifyingly, even though I knew it would happen, I blinked back tears. I felt an awful urge to lean into the pouting teenager bit, explain to these two people who were so wonderfully in love and had their lives together that it didn't surprise me, that Lily left. That she didn't want me enough for more than a hookup. No one ever did.

Well. I think you're gorgeous, Sam Bell.

I closed my eyes to block out the memory. Block out my friends' worried faces. They made the steel spine I had been trying to build feel more like a paper house. I wanted a greasy breakfast sandwich and hot chocolate and to maybe go back to bed for the rest of the day.

"You need to find her somehow," Claire said after a long moment, her voice determined. "There's no way you can sleep with Sam Bell and not be a little in love with them."

I managed a weak laugh.

"You don't have to pump me up, Claire. I'll be okay. I'm sorry I worried you."

"No, I'm serious!" she said. "I know you, Sam. You don't take relationships lightly. You should at least try to contact her, if you really like her, and see what she's thinking, too. Did she say anything to you before she left?"

"No. I just woke up and she was gone."

Kort sucked in a breath. "Ouch."

"Yeah," I agreed.

Claire frowned. "Do you know where she works or anything?"

"A vet clinic. Of which there are only, you know...a million, approximately, in this city."

Claire rolled her eyes. "There are not a million. And vet clinics have websites! That probably have employee pictures on them!"

"She's a receptionist," I said. "They probably don't have pictures of them." A pause. "Even though their jobs are really hard," I added.

Although, they had said Bri was one of the vets, right? They probably had pictures of the doctors.

The only thing I knew was that it couldn't be Simon and Garfunkel's vet, because I definitely would have remembered seeing Lily there.

I didn't say anything else. But mentally, I knew I was probably going to stalk every vet clinic within a thirty mile radius later tonight on my phone. Possibly over a pint of Ben & Jerry's.

"Alternately," Claire said, "We can just go to Moonie's *way* more than we have been, and wait to run into her. And ask her what the hell she was thinking."

I groaned. I hadn't even contemplated the possibility of running into Lily at Moonie's again one day. Why hadn't I thought about that? I truly was an idiot.

"My body feels like it's been hit by a truck," I countered. "You know our old asses can only handle Moonie's once every like, three months."

Claire pouted. "But I miss it. And I want to meet Lily."

I reached out and took her hand. "I'll think about it. And keep you updated. For now, can we talk about something else? Please?"

She squeezed my fingers. And then, because she was my best friend, she leaned back and said, "Sure."

And we did. And they made me laugh for a while, and I started to feel almost human. I was almost about to ask if they wanted to binge watch K-dramas or something, like we used to. And then Harry, who had been sleeping against Kort's chest this entire time except for a brief episode where he woke up and sucked on Claire's boob for a bit, woke up again, for real this time. Loud and *mad* at the world, and honestly, I could relate.

Claire grimaced.

"We should probably head out."

"Yeah, of course," I said quickly. Totally fine. I got it.

"But we'll hang out again soon?" she asked hopefully, and I could see in her face, that she knew I was disappointed. Or maybe she was disappointed. But this was what happened, when your friends all grew up better than you.

"Definitely." I actually lifted my body off the couch. It hurt. "Let me get a Harry hug before you go."

Kort handed him over, and he screamed in my face as I held him up, his little mouth so pink, his eyes so full of fury. I laughed and squeezed him to my chest anyway. He kicked me in the gut.

I knew I gave Claire and Kort a hard time about deciding to have kids. But sometimes, I really felt like Harry and I understood each other.

They all left then, and the apartment felt too empty, too quiet.

I ordered a pizza for myself and curled back up in bed. Garfunkel sank into the empty space next to me, where Lily had been last night. He was warm, and soft, but it wasn't the same.

I got out my phone.

I tried to empty my brain the best way I knew how. I watched a train make its slow way through the German countryside.

9

I SERIOUSLY CONTEMPLATED NOT GOING to work on Monday morning. I rarely called in sick. I deserved it.

But I knew it was simply delaying the inevitable. Jonny and Preeti and Bri would give me a hard time on Tuesday, instead. Best to rip off the Band-Aid. And I actually felt better, putting on my scrubs, doing my makeup, brushing my hair, like it was any other day. Like I had not spent all of yesterday afternoon in some kind of fugue state, my head and my heart trying to reconcile what I had done.

I couldn't tell if I was consumed with guilt, or with mourning. Or both.

Like most Monday mornings, it was busy at the clinic. Animals to help check in for surgery, phone calls to answer. Emails to respond to, records to send. A woman came in for a morning appointment with two new kittens, little black and white furballs we all got to cuddle and coo.

It wasn't my dream job, but it wasn't all bad, sometimes.

If luck was on my side, I would have been on a different lunch schedule today than everyone. But when I was finally able to collapse onto the saggy couch in the break room, Jonny and Preeti were there, finishing up their lunches.

"Girrrrl!" Jonny practically screamed.

"I'm dying, Lily." Preeti sat up in her chair. "DYING."

"I can't believe I missed the kiss!" Jonny moaned. "I am never leaving Moonie's early again."

"So did you bang?"

Jonny hit Preeti's shoulder.

"Preeti. Be decent." He leaned toward me. "But you know you could tell us, if you wanted to."

"I mean, *obviously* they banged," Preeti said.

I sighed. This was mortifying, but honestly it would be easiest to answer. Other than customer care, oversharing was our clinic's top skill. "Yes, we did."

Preeti squealed.

"So when are you seeing them again? God, you two were so precious."

"Oh." I dug my lunch out of my bag. "I'm not, probably?" I stood to busy myself by the microwave.

"What do you mean you're not?" Preeti sounded aghast.

I pressed the timer on the microwave and turned around, leaning my palms on the counter.

"Come on, you guys," I said. "You know Moonie's Lily isn't me. It was a special night, yeah. But it wasn't…" I shrugged. "Real."

They both frowned.

"What do you mean, it wasn't real?" Preeti asked. "I saw the way they looked at you all night, the way you looked at them."

I turned back around, trying to find a clean fork. They didn't get it.

And seriously, what the shit ever happened to all the forks in this place?

"Lily," Jonny tried, his voice sincere. "We all really liked them."

"Yeah," Preeti said. "We really did. They were fun, and sweet."

They *were* fun and sweet. And kind. And sexy.

I thought of their maps. The train videos. The way they looked at me at Moonie's.

And I thought they were also more full of longing than anyone else I'd ever met.

It made an ache form in my chest.

Maybe because it felt familiar.

Or maybe I was just upset because I didn't know if I'd ever be able to return to Moonie's again. Which broke my fucking heart.

"It was just an impulsive hookup," I insisted, stirring my noodles.

"But a *good* hookup, right?" Preeti asked. "Or was it not good?"

I shoved a forkful of noodles into my face.

"Very good," I said, mouth full, irritated.

"Lily!" Preeti shouted. "A good hookup with a fun, sweet person is a hookup you want to see again! Do you know how rough it is out there? I feel like I'm losing my mind right now. Back me up here, Jonny."

"Oh, you are fully backed up here. Lily, they were super into you, and super cute. Did something happen?"

I stared down into my bowl. *Did something happen?*

I couldn't keep on with this conversation. I knew how cold I sounded right now, how cruel and illogical it seemed like I was being.

But something *did* happen. And I didn't know when it happened, if it was when we sang "Jolene," or when I watched them dance with Preeti to "Like a Prayer," or if it was when they were taking off my bra and kissing down my spine. Or if it was when they answered all my prying questions half-asleep, and I wanted to stay curled up with my head on their shoulder, watching the boringest YouTube videos I had ever seen in my life, forever.

What happened was that I liked Sam Bell too much.

Extricating myself from them when they drifted off to sleep that morning, their phone falling onto their chest while that slow train still chugged through Serbia, was one of the hardest things I'd ever done. I had felt like a monster, leaving without a trace.

It was strange. I'd spent the first however many years of my life worrying that people would be so disgusted by my body that they would never love who I really was, *inside*. But I knew Sam wasn't disgusted by me: they had made me feel worshipped, desired, sexy, all night, both at Moonie's and in their apartment.

But what if it was the *inside* part that was actually disappointing?

How would Sam feel when they learned that the Lily who loved to sing and dance at Moonie's actually spent most of her time silently working at her sewing machine or reading a book? And even the sewing and reading days were good days; they were the days I wasn't so exhausted from the clinic that I could do something other than sit on the couch like a lump.

I imagined Sam would be sweet, and kind, and sexy, all the things they were now, for a while. I would, inevitably, fall for them even harder than I already had after only a few hours together. And then, eventually...they'd get bored. How wouldn't they? They wanted to travel the world; I barely made the rent in my shared apartment. They were full of dreams and I couldn't contribute in any way to fulfilling any of them.

It would break my heart, disappointing Sam Bell.

"Nothing happened," I said. "Look, can we talk about something else? Please? I don't mean to be a jerk; I'm just tired. Can we talk about Jonny and Pablo instead? Jonny SWVed for him, and then they left early! They obviously banged, too."

Jonny smiled slyly, twirling a bit in his swivel chair.

"Indeed."

Preeti rolled her eyes.

"Please, I already got all the deets from Jonny yesterday."

"He thought my performance was *sexy*," Jonny grinned.

"Of course he did," I smiled, genuinely, for the first time since walking into the room. "It *was*. It always is."

Preeti shoved her empty Tupperware back into her bag.

"And *Jonny* has another date with Pablo for next weekend. Because he doesn't hate happiness."

"All right, Preeti," Jonny gave her a look. "Let's leave Lily alone."

"Sorry, sorry." Preeti came over and squeezed me into an aggressive hug, almost knocking my noodles into my lap. "I just love you, Lily Bo Bily, you know?"

"I know." I patted her forearm.

"Either way," she stood with a sigh. "We *did* have an impressively high banging ratio this weekend."

Jonny nodded, taking his silverware to the sink. "We did."

"Go us!" Preeti pumped a fist into the air. "Maybe next time y'all can pass on some of your banging mojo to me."

"You can have all of mine," I said. "Although considering this weekend was the first time it worked, I can't make any promises."

"Banana nana fo Fily," Preeti shook her head at me on her way out the door. "You are chock full of banging mojo. Everyone knows it but you."

Jonny kissed my forehead. "But I think you do know it," he whispered, before following Preeti back into the treatment room.

I shoved two more bites of noodles into my mouth.

And then I threw the rest in the trash. My appetite had been off since Saturday night. Maybe I'd never drink gin again. Maybe this was an opportunity to better myself.

I spent the rest of my lunch break walking around the block, kicking away leaves with my sneakers, listening to nothing but the wind whistling through the trees, surrounded by the sure safety of silence.

But in between the quiet, all I could hear was a scratchy, off-key voice singing *turn around, bright eyes.*

It was ridiculous. And I could say what I wanted to Preeti and Jonny. To myself.

But no matter what I did, I couldn't get it out of my head.

THREE DAYS LATER, on my drive home Thursday night, it happened. Finally, another song barged into my consciousness. Finally, another song forced me to wake up.

"This Charming Man" was on my radio.

While I *had* vaguely recognized it at Moonie's on Saturday night, I couldn't remember the last time I had actually heard it for real. It piped loudly into the quiet confines of my car, just me and the dark night and Morrissey. And while I wasn't a superstitious person, I couldn't help but feel it was a sign.

I turned the volume up even louder and allowed myself to think about teenaged Sam listening in their bedroom. It was melancholy and beautiful. A lump formed in my throat.

I realized it all at once, listening to that song. I had been correct, essentially, in my assessment of Saturday night. Sam and I barely knew each other, and then we slept together. It was a hookup.

But even though there was so much I didn't know about them—what was their family like? Had they grown up here? What was their favorite movie, favorite childhood memory?—maybe, somehow, in those few hours at Moonie's, we had been able to see the essence of each other. Through the music we loved, the way our bodies moved and touched, how easy it was to talk about the things that mattered. Like through a few pop songs we were able to understand who we had been, who we dreamed of being, and the possibility of who we could be now—at least who we could be in those rare, important moments when we let ourselves go.

And maybe holding that night tight to my chest forever, because I was scared of what would happen if we tried to pursue anything further, could be beautiful in its own bittersweet way. Romantic, even. One perfect night preserved in memory, untamed and untainted.

But maybe I deserved more. Maybe Sam—both the person who had listened to The Smiths too much, and the person who collected maps and made me come so hard I almost blacked out—deserved more, too. Maybe we could fill in the details later. Maybe when someone saw the essence of you, it would be wrong to let that go.

When I got home, I almost frantically Googled, my heart pounding. It was so easy to find them. They popped right up on the university's website. Sam Bell: Current

Class Schedule. Office Hours. University email and phone number.

And a picture. Those eyes. My stomach flipped.

Office Hours.

That could work.

Without even taking off my scrubs, I turned on the desk lamp over my sewing machine. I got out my sketch-book. And I began to plan.

Maybe Bold Lily could, for the first time in her life, attempt to make an appearance outside of The Moonlight Café. In broad daylight, at least once.

I thought about—for perhaps the hundredth time that week—what it had felt like to sing "Jolene" with Sam, how much raw joy had filled my veins.

Go for it, Lily.

It was what Dolly would do.

10

LILY & SAM

THE FOLLOWING TUESDAY, I stood in front of a plain wooden door and took a deep breath. And then another. I stared at the placard in the window: *Sam Bell*. The letters made shivers run down my arms. So they hadn't been a figment of my imagination. Good to know.

The whole time I'd been walking through the halls, up the stairs here to the third floor, I'd expected someone to stop me, tell me I didn't belong. But no one had even looked at me. And now I was here.

And I was terrified.

Okay. *Okay.* I was doing this.

I brought my hand up, made a fist, practiced. I wanted it to sound strong.

KNOCK

KNOCK

KNO—

The door opened before I'd even finished my practiced number of knocks, my knuckles suspended in midair.

"Hey Eric, did you for—"

Sam's mouth hung open, their eyes widening as they

took me in. Realized I wasn't Eric. My breath got stuck in my throat.

"Lily?"

I barreled inside before I could lose my nerve.

I dumped the bag in my hand into the empty chair in the corner, the only seat other than the one at their desk. There was barely enough room in here for us both to stand; if someone actually sat in that empty chair while Sam sat at theirs, their knees would knock together. Coming to office hours as a student must have been terrifying.

Even when you weren't about to make a potential romantic catastrophe out of yourself.

"Hi," I said, turning around to finally look at them.

And oh. *Oh.*

I had been so preoccupied the last several days working on what I'd brought here today, practicing what I was going to say, convincing myself I could do this at all. Focused on the task at hand. I always liked having a project.

But now that Sam was actually in front of me, everything came rushing back.

The first moment our eyes locked across the room at Moonie's. Their hand on my knee under the table. Shoving them against the wall in the parking lot. Their mouth on my earlobe, their mouth on my back. Their mouth on my clit. How it felt when they finally pounded into me, over and over and over, so full and right.

I had expected their office to be sterile. A cubicle, maybe. But the only light in the room emanated from a lamp on Sam's desk, casting everything—casting Sam—in a warm, golden glow.

I wanted to climb them like a tree.

"Hi," they said, shoving their hands in their pockets. "Um. Why are you here, Lily?"

I blinked. *Focus, Lily.*

And after a few more vigorous blinks, I truly took in Sam's face.

I had been ready for a look of confusion or surprise. But what threw me was the wariness I found there instead. Their face had been relaxed and happy when they'd opened the door expecting Eric, but now, it had closed off completely. Like they couldn't wait for this to be over.

My stomach sank down to my toes.

"A couple things," I said, trying to sound upbeat, normal. Like I hadn't been thinking about this moment for days. Like my palms weren't sweating.

I glanced quickly at the walls around us as I tried to gather breath—and courage—into my lungs. The maps here all seemed more old-time-y than the majority of the ones at Sam's apartment, mostly of the Eastern seaboard, Europe. But they were nicely framed, neatly arranged on the wall, just as at their home.

I thought about how when Sam talked, they made it sound like they were a mess inside. *Bumbling through*, I remembered them saying at Moonie's.

But all of the hard evidence that surrounded them suggested that in reality, Sam Bell treated their life with extreme care.

"So. I made you some clothes." I nodded toward the bag. "I had to guess on your measurements, so they might all be shit anyway, but…" Another deep breath. "It was fun for me. I like making clothes for people, and I liked making clothes for you. Sitting at my sewing table, where I feel safest. Thinking of you."

I swallowed.

"But, after they were done, I realized they might not be

the nice gesture I'd thought they'd be. Clothes are personal, Sam. You should always have the right to wear what makes *you* feel good, and it's entirely possible one conversation wasn't enough for me to know, accurately, what makes you feel good. So, I, um. Brought a backup gift, too. If you don't want the clothes."

Sam eyed me levelly, leaning their palms back against their desk. There was an uncomfortable moment of silence.

"You made me clothes," they said slowly.

"Yeah." I swallowed again. "I'm sorry. You really don't have to take them."

Another long pause. I forced myself to not melt into a puddle.

"I...I'm sorry, Lily. But why are you bringing me gifts?"

"I wanted to explain myself. And thought if you didn't let me, which would be within your rights, I could at least leave something with you. For you. As a thank you for a truly wonderful night."

They stared at me a minute more. And maybe my own eyes were going wobbly, but I thought their face softened, just a tiny bit.

"I'd like to see the clothes," they said eventually, and I about fainted with relief.

I moved to the bag and took out the sweater.

"We could start with this," I said, turning around, the fabric soft and reassuring in my hands. It was 10% cashmere. The most I could afford. The feel and weight of it leant me confidence I desperately needed, being that I was starting to doubt myself more with each passing second.

And then I looked up and actually processed Sam's outfit.

It was like my brain could only take in Sam in bits and pieces today, or something, but—

"Oh *no*, Sam," I couldn't help myself from blurting. "That shirt's awful."

Sam blinked and looked down at themselves. And then nodded their head, once.

"I know," they said.

It was a short-sleeved linen button-down shirt, a boring pale plaid, and it might have been fine, if it wasn't a size too big and wrinkled as shit.

I took a step forward. I was pretty sure I was shaking a little. But this was my one shot. Bold Lily had to try.

I raised my hands to the first button, my fingers an inch from their chin.

"Can I?"

I looked up. Watched Sam suck in a small breath.

And after an excruciating moment, they answered, almost in a whisper: "Yes."

Oh thank god. My heart beat harder with each button, but I rid Sam of that horrible shirt. Resisted the urge to run my hands over their skin.

And then I lifted the sweater over their head.

"Oh, damn," they said, pulling their arms through the sleeves. "Soft."

"Yes," I whispered, and I gave in to the urge, like it was acceptable now that there was new fabric there. I ran my palms over their shoulders, down their chest, rested them on their belly. The sweater was dark purple, the perfect amount of fuzzy, and actually fit Sam's body, so you could see their curves. "Soft."

We stood like that, practicing our best move—staring at each other too long—until I removed my hands and turned back to the bag.

"We don't have to do the next part," I said, holding the folded up leggings and skirt. "You can take them home and try them on later. And then burn them. Whatever you want. Your decision."

Sam looked at me, then at the clock. They reached over and locked the door, checked that the blinds were pulled tight.

"Office hours are over," they said. "Let's do it."

When they pulled their jeans down, I saw the angry red lines they left on their skin, and I bit my lip. I knew this entire exercise was perhaps more for my benefit than Sam's. That not everyone cared about clothing, put so much emotional investment in it as I did. But I could not wait until Sam's skin was covered with soft, stretchy, rayon-cotton blend instead, a fabric that held their body in with care instead of punishment.

I handed over the bundle of clothes. Watched quietly as they pulled on the forest green leggings. The charcoal grey pencil skirt, dotted with small white polka dots.

I had to bite back my pride. My guesswork on fit had been even better than I hoped.

They looked divine.

But Sam only looked down at themselves and sighed.

"Oh," I said, blinking back sudden tears, feeling absolutely ridiculous that they had appeared at all. "It's okay Sam! It's okay if it's not transformative, if they don't fit. I'll take them back. You can keep the sweater, it's—"

"Lily," they interrupted, shaking their head. I thought maybe they were smiling, just a little, but my brain was panicking too much to fully believe I wasn't making it up. "Stop. Okay? Breathe. It's okay. I like them. They feel good. It's just...as I thought."

They ran their hand over the top of the skirt, where it hugged the soft bottom of their belly.

Oh. Okay.

My brain recalculated, and I couldn't help myself. I reached out, covered their hand with mine.

"I like that," I said. "That's your body, Sam. That's just how it's shaped. There's nothing wrong with it."

Their eyes met mine. My own body felt overly aware of everything: the pulse in my fingertip, pressing against Sam's knuckle. The slight unsteadiness of my breathing. The way Sam's lips were just barely parted. How small their office was, that glow from their lamp. It felt like we could have been a tiny pod, rocketing toward outer space, no one else around but us.

I stepped back.

Trying to steady my breath, I turned around and reached once again into the bag.

"I brought an alternate, though."

I brought out a different skirt: same charcoal gray, although this one was patterned with little pink lightning bolts. The cut was still simple, but more free flowing, with an asymmetrical hem.

I could tell as soon as Sam slipped it on that this one felt better to them. They swung their hips a bit. They were staring down at themselves, and the light was dim. But I was pretty sure they were blushing.

"Swishy," they said. "Fun."

I exhaled. Swishy seemed promising.

I still wasn't entirely sure if this was going well, or if everything was awful.

But time to stop messing around now.

I took a tiny step forward.

"Sam," I said. "I'm sorry."

They looked up, and there was a spark there, in their eyes—did they truly like the clothes? But whatever it was faded. Their eyes were steady on mine as hurt came to the surface instead.

"You said a few minutes ago that you had a wonderful night," they said quietly. "So why did you leave?"

I closed my eyes. *Here we go.*

"I feel like you got to know me under false pretenses, Sam," I said, snapping my eyes back open to look at them. "The person you see at karaoke, who dances and sings loudly and confidently is...not me. She only exists at Moonie's. The truth is that in my everyday life, I'm..." I shrugged. "Quiet. Kind of boring. I didn't want you to actually get to know me and...be disappointed."

Their eyes narrowed.

"Wait a second," they said. "I thought you yelled at *me* for calling myself boring."

"You're *not*," I said defiantly. "You're a *professor*. You have this badass little office." I waved my hands around to make my point. "I would kill to have a little office like this, all to myself."

"You make your own clothes," Sam countered. "You knew how to make *me* clothes."

"You studied abroad in *Rome*," I shot back.

"You have this *voice*," Sam said. "This voice that..." They faltered. "Slays me."

My breath caught. I blinked, a gap of silence stretching a moment too long.

"You have two cats named Simon and Garfunkel," I managed. "Which is really fucking charming."

"You have cool, interesting friends who love and support you," they said.

"And my middle name is Marie!" I threw my hands in the air. "Why are we shouting facts about each other?"

"I don't know," Sam said, but they were smiling. I was sure now. It was possible they had been smiling this whole time. "Although I'm pretty sure you started it. My middle name is Anthony, by the way. After my grandfather on my mom's side."

Ridiculously, I felt like crying again.

"Well," I said. "Well, that's nice to know. I want to know stuff like that. I just…" I shook my head, trying to get back to the point. "Saturday night was intense. And my past relationships have not always been awesome, and it felt like…things could potentially be awesome, with you."

"Yeah," Sam said, face sobering. "We're agreed, there."

"And it's…scary," I ended, and wow, that sounded twenty times more embarrassing coming out of my mouth than I had anticipated. And I had anticipated it being pretty fucking embarrassing. "And I don't want to be scared. So I just want you to know who I really am, that I'm not actually Karaoke Lily, before we go any further. If you want to go any further."

There. I didn't know if I had said anything exactly how my heart wanted to say it, but I'd said enough.

I felt suddenly tired.

Sam released a small sigh.

They pushed off from their desk and took my face in their hands.

"Lily," they said affectionately, running a thumb over my cheek. "Of course Karaoke Lily is who you are."

I started to protest, but they put a finger to my mouth.

"I mean, if we were all who we are at Moonie's all the time, we'd all be exhausted." They smiled that gentle smile. "You can't fake who you are when you're up on that dance floor with a microphone in your hand, Lily. It wouldn't turn me on so much if it was fake. It might not be who you are seven days a week, but that doesn't mean it's not still a part of who you are." They studied me, their eyes serious. "Look. Right before you came in here? This freshman,

Eric, who's only taking my intro class to fulfill an elective requirement, who thought it'd be an easy A, stopped by to tell me how much more he was enjoying the class than he thought he would."

They paused, brow creasing.

"Okay, and to ask me for an extension on his next paper, because his grandma died. *But* he also had all these questions about the Dawes Act, which is understandable because the Dawes Act was fucking wild, but the fact that he was asking the questions, outside of class, that he *felt* something about injustice in 1887—"

Sam was still holding on to my face, and I didn't know if they even noticed that they started squeezing my skin tighter as they talked, but—well, I liked it. A lot.

"Anyway," they huffed out a breath. "Moments like that are *my* Moonie's moments, you know? And they only happen every once in a while. I wish I could be a brilliant professor for them, for you, all the time, but I'm not. I know, though, at this point, that if I don't let myself feel a *little* proud of Eric de la Rosa being real pissed off about the Dawes Act, I won't have the energy to keep going."

One of their hands caressed down my neck. Involuntarily, my eyes fluttered closed.

"Sorry," they said. "I'm still running on a slight high from Eric. I just meant...we have to take our wins, Lily. You at Moonie's?" I felt them lean in, their breath hot on my cheek. "You simply wouldn't be able to sing like that if that voice wasn't yours."

What would Dolly and Carrie do? I asked myself.

What would Karaoke Lily have done, Saturday night?

And I thought—maybe—they'd all want me to look at Sam, and believe them.

"Plus," Sam murmured into my temple, "You weren't very quiet at my apartment, either."

I flushed.

"That was different, too," I said, weakly.

"Mm." They kissed my forehead. "Either way, I find it very hard to believe that you will disappoint me. Show me your quiet parts, Lily. You have no idea how much I would like to be maybe-a-little-boring together."

They kissed my nose. It was sweet, and tender.

But at that moment, I did not feel like being very tender at all.

~

LILY LEANED her head back to look at me. I thought—I hoped—I saw something like possibility there in those brown eyes. Something like trust. Something like want.

And then she reached up and kissed me with a ferocity that made my head spin.

Her arms were suddenly around me, clawing at my back, and I stumbled half a step, until my butt was fully pushed back against the desk.

Just like last time, as soon as her lips were against mine, our bodies aligned, it was like we just...fit. Like our bodies were meant to be together: my softness next to hers; her strength bleeding into me. And within minutes, my entire system buzzed with need.

Although it was possible I'd been buzzing with need ever since she walked in the door, considering she looked so ridiculously fantastic. Her hair was down today, and she was wearing a leggings-skirt combo too, although her skirt was long and pale and floofy and made of...what was that fabric? Tulle? Almost opaque but not quite, a little magical, like fairies had concocted it in an enchanted forest. It was offset by a faded Sinead O'Connor t-shirt, tight against her chest, and a thick cardigan sweater. A cozy infinity scarf wrapped around her neck. A perfect picture: Lily in the Fall. I wanted to cuddle her to death.

Except when she first walked in, I told myself I didn't. Because I had spent the last week and a half convincing myself this was over, that *all* of this was over: Lily and everything she represented. I had gathered all my strength, and decided to *not* virtually stalk every veterinary clinic in the metropolitan area. I had caught up on all my grading, instead. Apparently taught the shit out of the Dawes Act. Smiled extra hard at my barista. Told myself I was fine.

And I was. I would be. Because I would always have my friends. Claire would take care of me when I was old and fragile. We'd already promised each other, years ago. And if Claire died first, I was sure Kort would take care of me, albeit more grudgingly. Or if all else failed, Harry. I'd make sure he knew his responsibilities, once he was old enough to talk. In any case, I didn't need...need.

But when Lily started to explain that the reason she walked out of my apartment two Sundays ago was because of *her*, and not *me*...it knocked the wind out of me a little. I didn't know why I had been so surprised. Maybe I was a little self-absorbed. Or maybe my head was still more fucked from Dan than I realized. Because Dan made it pretty clear that it was me. That it was always me who had misinterpreted things. Who wasn't the right fit, who wasn't enough.

The fact that Lily might think *she* wasn't enough had honestly never even occurred to me.

It made all of my not-so-stable walls crumble immediately.

Because it was going to be the most fun I'd ever had, proving her wrong.

I pulled away from her mouth to 1) breathe, and 2) remove that scarf from her neck. The collar of her t-shirt was ripped and loose, and a growly sound escaped my throat, pleased at all that newly exposed, available skin. I attacked it with my tongue, with my teeth, and she wove her fingers into my hair, grabbing and pulling with a delirious-making amount of gentle pressure.

"Lily," I said into her shoulder, my own hands roaming under her sweater, and then under her t-shirt, for which she rewarded me with a gasp, "I thought I'd never see you again."

"Sam," she whispered, and I thought that was all. I was seconds away, myself, from whispering her own name, over and over, for no other reason than wanting to say it. But then, a minute later, just as I was about to suck her earlobe into my mouth, she added: "I missed you."

For a fraction of a second, I froze. And then, without really thinking about it, I found myself gathering up all that magical tulle in my hands, until my fingers could reach between those wonderful thighs. She shifted her legs, opening for me, and I pressed my fingers against her, and she was so hot there, even through the layers of thin fabric.

"Yes," she whispered, tilting her hips toward me, "Please, Sam. Touch me."

I always was a good listener.

Using both hands, I separated her leggings and underwear from her skin, navigating one hand down, down, and *oh*. I sucked in a short breath when I felt how wet she already was. Her underwear was some type of satiny material, smooth and cool against my knuckles, contrasted against the heat of her. She made soft, breathy sounds against my neck, and I wanted to swallow them whole.

After a few minutes of circling her clit, I slowly slid one finger inside her. She ground against my palm.

"Sam," she whispered, "That's perfect."

She had sort of collapsed into me, so it was hard to see

her face, but I leaned down to plant a kiss at the edge of her eye, where a few locks of hair had fallen forward and gotten stuck on her mascara. I moved another finger inside, and then another. She moaned, one of her hands tickling up my side, underneath this soft, soft sweater. This sweater she had made for me.

I didn't quite understand what I had done to deserve any of this. But maybe now wasn't the time to overthink it. Maybe now was the time to do what I always tried to do at Moonie's: let myself go. Feel grateful as hell to be alive in this moment, right now.

And let everything else fall away.

Lily was leaning back, mumbling something incoherent: "I need—I can't—"

She grabbed my plaid linen shirt, which was crumpled on the desk behind me. The shirt that I knew was ill-fitting and too wrinkled, that I really wished I had not worn today. Not that I could have anticipated Lily showing up at my office door.

But then she shoved her face in the shirt to muffle her cry as she tightened around my fingers and came, the same cry I remembered so well from that Saturday night, somehow feral and pretty all at once. And on second thought, maybe I would frame the shirt.

She dropped it to the ground as she came down, leaning even more heavily into me. I extricated my hand and used my other to draw small circles on her back. We were quiet a moment. Absently, I rubbed my thumb against my forefinger with my free hand, feeling her slickness that was still there, taking the time to really absorb it, along with the general warmth of her body against mine, the slight scratchiness of her sweater on the fingertips of my left hand. So many pleasurable sensations, so many different textures. So many ways to be in a body.

A bit shakily, Lily pushed herself away from me. Silently, she repeated the same actions to me that I had done to her.

She lifted up my skirt, rumpling it up on my stomach. She gave me one small squeeze through my leggings, and I was so riled up, that was honestly almost enough to send me over the edge. But I got a hold of myself—or rather, Lily made quick work of pulling down my leggings and briefs and taking hold of me.

For one brief, glorious moment. And then she was gone.

I opened my eyes, which apparently I had closed at some point, probably when she lifted up my skirt. But it was a good thing I opened them again, because I got to witness Lily reaching underneath her own skirt, and...rummaging around in there for a second, before bringing her hand out again. She grabbed the base of my cock again, this time semi-lubed with her own release.

She looked up at me and laughed a little. Probably because the look on my face was likely...something.

"Better than spit," she said.

"That it is," I concurred.

"Shut up," she said, blushing suddenly, and for some reason it was that blush that made me remember we were in my fucking *office*. Holy shit.

I forgot again two seconds later. Because she reached her other hand into my hair and brought me down to kiss her as she rubbed me to oblivion. And that *mouth*. Those hands. That tongue, that—

"Lily," I broke away. It was getting to be too much, so fast. So fucking dirty and good. I felt out of my mind. "What's your last name?"

"Fischer," she huffed, looking down in concentration.

I was able to get out, "I missed you, too, Lily Marie Fischer," before—

"Oh *fuck*. Wait. Fuck." I gripped her hand, stopping her. She gave me a quizzical look. I had to pant a few times before I was able to explain. "Don't," huff, "want to ruin," huff, "the sweater."

It occurred to me later that I could have just taken off the damn sweater, but it was fine. Because with a smile, Lily sunk to her knees instead, and then I wasn't able to form words. To be honest, her mouth had barely even covered the head of my cock when I exploded. I didn't need a shirt to scream into—my entire system always seemed to freeze when I came and I could only get out the faintest groans; I was slightly jealous of Lily's ability to make such a joyful sound—but it seemed to last forever. I felt almost bad. But Lily appeared to be doing just fine. She leaned her head against my thigh when I was done, and we both took a breather.

I really had missed her, I realized. I had spent every day since she'd left my apartment convincing myself I didn't. I tried so hard I believed myself. But now that she was here, it was like rediscovering something I had held once, however briefly, that made me feel so very light, so full of joy. Something my entire being had been longing to find. And I wasn't going to let go this time.

I pulled up the leggings, readjusted my skirt. Lily stood to meet me again. I glanced at her.

"Um." I hesitated. "We're probably doing things a little backwards here, but...would you want to get dinner with me tonight?"

Her face cracked into a smile. She relaxed against me.

"Yes," she said. It was possible my heart soared.

"Tacos?" I asked. She snuggled even closer.

"Tacos," she agreed.

I ran my fingers through her hair.

"Perhaps not *so* boring, you and me," I murmured.

"Maybe," she said. But there was a smile in it.

"Although I do have to admit this wasn't quite typical for my office hours."

She muffled a half-laugh, half-hum into my shoulder.

The memory of today might actually prove to be a problem. I would have to work on not getting turned on every time I entered my office now. But that was a problem for Future Sam.

"Hey," I said, some of her words from earlier poking through my post-orgasmic haze. "Hey. Didn't you say you had brought a backup gift?"

She leaned away. "I did."

"Can I have it?" I asked, feeling eager and happy in such a blissfully simple way. Like somehow, for some reason, Christmas had arrived early for me today, out of the blue: love and light and gratitude. And presents.

Lily cocked her head, considering. "Will you buy my tacos?"

"Of course."

She grinned. "Okay. But don't get too excited or anything."

"Well, now I'm *really* excited." I pumped my fist. "*Back - up - gift! Back - up - gift!*"

"Okay, okay." She disentangled herself from me. "But, uh. Can I wash my hands first?"

"Yeah." I smiled. "There's a bathroom right across the hall." I leaned over to unlock the door. I probably should have washed my hands too. But some perverse part of me wanted to keep Lily's scent on me a little longer.

As I waited for her to come back, I stared at the walls of my tiny office, taking a deep breath. I swished my skirt a few times. It was nice.

I would need to wear it more, to figure out if I actually liked it or not. If it truly fit. But I was glad to have it as an option. Maybe some people were able to figure everything out on their own. But someone showing me different options had always been so helpful to me. Even if it took me a while to grab onto the things that made sense for me, that felt good, until they actually felt like my own.

They were small things, in the end. Pronouns were such tiny words. A dab of makeup, when I felt like it. A different piece of fabric.

But it was so nice. Having options.

When Lily came back, she walked immediately to her bag again without looking at me. She lifted something out and hid it behind her back.

"This might be dumb," she said, biting her lip.

"Lily," I said. "New rule. No more trashing your gifts before you give them to me, okay? It sort of dampens the whole experience a bit."

"You're right. You're right. Okay."

She took a step forward.

"I made you a map."

She handed me the frame.

It was small, maybe 8x10.

I couldn't stop smiling. I felt it lighting up my face, unstoppable.

The Moonlight Café, it said at the top.

She had included all the best parts, with neat little labels. Of course she could draw; of course she had wonderful handwriting. All of those parts of the brain that I could never get to light up were bright and beautiful in hers.

Behind the bar, there was a small figure labeled *Hot, Scary Bartender*. I laughed.

"You think the bartender is hot?"

"Oh yeah," Lily answered, with feeling, and shivered a little.

But I couldn't even feel jealous. Because while the map was mostly drawn in black pen, there were small red hearts drawn in every spot that had mattered the most on Saturday night: *Sad Sam Table*, as she had labeled it, in the corner. The spot by the bar where we had talked about clothes and Morrissey. The middle of the dance floor, next to the microphone.

"I love it," I said.

"Yeah?" Her eyes were wide, hopeful.

"So much." I had never loved something this hard in my goddamn life.

"I know it's not, like, a work of art or anything."

"Lily. It's the best. *The best.* I already know where I'm going to put it."

She opened her mouth, and I knew she was going to say something else self-deprecating. But instead, she only said, "Okay," and smiled.

"Thank you." I let out a breath. "I don't know if anyone has ever been this nice to me in my life."

Lily frowned. "Well." She turned around, picked up the empty bag and her purse. "We are going to have to fix that."

I picked up my black jean jacket from the hook on the wall. Threw my own bag over my shoulder, shoved my jeans and old shirt inside. I smoothed my hands over my skirt and then joined Lily where she waited, in front of my office door.

"Oh my god," she breathed, looking at me. "Sam. Your jacket."

"Yeah?" I looked down, worried I had accidentally put it on inside out or something.

"It's perfect. It makes the whole outfit—"

ANITA KELLY

She moved her hands around rapidly, and actually *squealed* a little, bouncing on the balls of her feet.

"Gah!" she eventually shouted. "You look so good!"

I laughed. And held the Moonie's map to my chest.

"I might change for dinner," I said, hoping that wouldn't disappoint her. "I don't know yet."

Lily reached over and squeezed my hand, the one not clutching the best present ever.

"That's fine by me. As long as you throw out that other shirt."

"Oh, no. You screamed into it when you were coming. I'm never getting rid of it now. Anyway, this is probably the bigger deal than dinner, wearing this down the hall right now," I rambled, thinking out loud as it hit me. "My colleagues or students could see me. Which...actually doesn't feel like that big of a deal, now that I think about it?"

Lily waited patiently.

"And since I was very recently sexed, there's not much threat of sporting a woody in these leggings—which *are* very comfortable, by the way—so that's good."

Lily made a choking sound.

"A woody?"

"I know, I know, I'm feeling kind of loopy and it just popped out. My grandpa used to call them that."

"Grandpa Anthony?"

"Yes!" I smiled. "He was a very dirty old man."

"I do think plenty of people with penises wear skirts and dresses every day and manage just fine, Sam."

"You're right. I'm being weird."

"No. You're processing. And being cute."

"Yeah?" I opened the door. "How cute? Like, invite-me-back-to-your-place-after-tacos cute?"

Lily bit her lip. "My place is a mess, and I have two roommates and thin walls. I like your place better."

"You *do* have to see where I put my newest map," I conceded. "Although I want to know more about your roommates. And, you know, everything else about you."

We walked into the hall. No one even looked at us, which was strange, because I was pretty sure we were both glowing.

"Did you drive?" I asked. She shook her head.

"No, I took the bus."

"Cool." I gave her hand a small squeeze. "I could drive you home, if you wanted? And we can meet back up in a few hours?"

"Yeah. I'd like that."

"Holy shit, I cannot wait to see what your taco order is."

She laughed.

"I'm serious," I said. "But don't tell me. I want it to be a surprise."

She made another little giggly noise, and I looked over at her. She was looking down at the ground, shaking her head. And smiling.

Romantic prowess: not bad, actually.

"Hey," I said as we exited the building, headed to the employee lot. "Serious question."

"Shoot."

I stopped in the middle of the sidewalk and turned to face her.

"Would you sing for me sometimes? Like, if I continue to be cute enough to get you back in my apartment?"

Her cheeks went pink, her eyes surprised.

"Like...just hanging out in your apartment, singing? A capella?"

I shrugged, tugging her a little closer.

"Yeah. You know, when we're in bed, or making hot chocolate in the kitchen...maybe you'd sing 'Dream a Little Dream of Me' and I'd boop some whipped cream onto your nose. Or something. Not that I have fantasized about this or anything."

She covered her face with her hands. But I could tell she was still smiling.

"I don't know," she said through her fingers. "I might have to work up to that."

Oh my god. She hadn't been lying. She was...shy.

And it was absolutely, thrillingly adorable.

"That's okay." I stepped back. Gave my skirt a little twirl. Because I was feeling full of possibility, my body a tiny bit more free. "No pressure."

She dropped her hands and we kept walking.

"I *am* okay with one thing," she said after a minute.

"Yeah?" I looked over.

"Singing along to the radio." She grinned. "The inside of a car is definitely the best place for singing, outside of Moonie's."

"Oh my god." I grabbed her hand again and started jogging toward my beat up Corolla. "Let's fucking go."

"Okay, okay," she laughed as we got there, out of breath. "But I get to choose the station. And warn me next time you're going to make me run like that; my boobs are angry at you now."

"You're on, Fischer."

I unlocked the door and threw my bag in the backseat.

"And I'll make it up to your boobs later," I added as I put the keys in the ignition.

She snapped her seatbelt into place.

"Deal."

I turned the engine.

And then I waited for Lily to sing me a song.

ACKNOWLEDGMENTS

This is a little story, but I still have big-sized gratitude for many people who contributed to it and gave me the courage to publish it. Thank you:

Em Roberts, for the gorgeous cover which captures all three main characters: Sam, Lily, and Lily's dress. Piper Vossy, Jen St. Jude, Manda Bednarik, Kate Cochrane, and Chandra Fisher for your valuable feedback, editing, and friendship. Matthew Broberg-Moffitt and Sossity Chiricuzio, thank you for your kindness and encouragement.

My Fork Family, who get me through every day, and especially the self-pub Forkies, who helped inspire me to do this.

Mom, for all those trips to the fabric store, no matter how much we whined about them at the time. You are my favorite fashion designer.

Kathy, for being the best "Sweet Child O' Mine" duet partner, and the best partner in all things.

Finally, thank you to you, for reading this queer karaoke love story! I wrote this novella at the height of the COVID pandemic in 2020, when I was missing the friendship and magic of public spaces like Moonie's, and needed to remind myself that they existed, and will exist again, one day. Writing it brought me necessary escape and joy; I hope you found even a fraction of both in Sam and Lily's story.

If you did like their story, it would mean so much to me if you left a review for this novella on your preferred review site, or recommended it to a friend.

If you are interested in more queer love stories from me, sign up for my newsletter on anitakellywrites.com, or follow me for updates on Twitter @daffodilly or Instagram @anitakellywrites.

For now, keep reading for sneak peaks of the next story from Moonie's, and my upcoming full-length debut release!

(SUPER) SNEAK PEAK OF OUR FAVORITE SONGS

Return to the world of The Moonlight Café in Fall 2021 with *Our Favorite Songs*, a new queer karaoke novella which asks the important questions, such as: what happens when you get snowed in with the high school crush you haven't seen in five years?

Chapter One

Aiden

"OF COURSE," KAI ANDREWS SAID as he sat down across from me. "It's you."

Kai Andrews.

Just sat down.

Across from me.

I did a quick memory check to make sure I wasn't high.

Nope. The only depressant I'd consumed tonight was this just-okay IPA in front of me. And Kai Andrews was definitely still sitting at my table, snug against the back wall of Moonie's, next to the sole window in the entire building. Which was mostly obscured by a large neon sign advertising Bud Light. It was the table where I was supposed to be meeting Penelope, my best friend, for our semi-annual let's-get-drunk-and-laugh-at-people-doing-karaoke Moonie's invitational.

Which my high school nemesis had definitely never, ever been invited to.

~

SNEAK PEAK OF LOVE & OTHER DISASTERS

Want more messy queers and non-binary love interests? Read on for a sneak peak of *Love & Other Disasters*, my full-length debut out from Forever Publishing in January 2022.

∼

Chapter 1

DAHLIA WOODSON MIGHT HAVE BEEN shit at marriage, but she could dice an onion like a goddamn professional.

The first even slices, the cross hatching. The comfort in how logical and perfect it was. Dahlia had put in the work, onion after onion, until she could create consistent knife cuts every time. Until she trusted her hand, her knife, without having to think about it at all: fast and efficient and right.

When Dahlia stepped onto the set of Chef's Special in Burbank, California on a Tuesday morning in late July, she thought about onions.

She certainly couldn't focus on the mahogany floor

under her feet, how it positively *gleamed*. Or how high the ceilings were, far higher than she had imagined, higher than seemed necessary. Like some sort of sports stadium. For food nerds.

And the lights—sweet holy Moses.

It felt like walking into an airport terminal after a long, cross-country flight: everything too fast, too loud, too full of *new*.

Except the set of Chef's Special wasn't new, not exactly. Dahlia had seen it before, back home on her TV set. But it was different in person. Her brain struggled to process that any of this was real, that this was actually happening.

She walked around the soaring wooden archway which marked the rear edge of the set. It was majestic and unmistakable, like the doorway of a cathedral, if a kitchen could be a church.

She was busy staring at the archway in awe, dazzled by the shining lights above.

Which was why a second later, she smacked herself right into a soft, solid wall of person.

A person who released a displeased grunt at Dahlia's face implanting into their chest.

Dahlia bounced back a step, a rubber ball of embarrassment, her tongue sticking to the roof of her mouth. Looking up, she saw the other contestant run a freckled hand through their hair, which was buzz cut on the sides, longer on top. Their hand released, and a flop of strawberry blonde locks fell back over their right eyebrow.

Dahlia cleared five feet, but barely. And this person was *tall*. Meaning that eyebrow hovered what felt like a full floor above her.

But it was cute, the strawberry hair. It made Dahlia think of leaves changing color in the fall, and Anne of

Green Gables, and sunsets reflected off of still water. They hadn't moved at all since her face met their chest, and the nearness of another body felt grounding somehow, like when your eyes lock onto someone in Arrivals you recognize, the cacophony of the airport finally settling around you.

And so maybe it was the sunset hair or the simple proximity of another sentient human being, but Dahlia opened her mouth and—

"Oh, god. I just ran right the fuck into you. I am so, so sorry. I am just so nervous. Like, I think the last time I was this nervous was at my fourth-grade spelling bee, when I forgot how to spell 'whistle' and everyone laughed at me and I maybe peed my tights, just a little. God, wearing tights is the *worst*."

Dahlia saw, from the corner of her eye, the other eleven contestants milling around while a producer named Janet began herding them to their assigned cooking stations. Strawberry Blonde Hair kept standing there, staring at her with a blank look on their face. Likely wondering what was wrong with her. Dahlia felt awkward ending the conversation here, but she also didn't know how to transition smoothly from fourth grade urination— although, for the record, she stood by her assessment of tights—so she simply barreled on, her brain scrambling to find a more relevant way to finish this horrifying minute of her life.

"This is weird, right? That we are going to like, be on TV. That this is real. All I can think about is onions, which is so dumb because everyone else is probably thinking about, you know, veal and foie gras or whatever. Although I'm also thinking about how I'm probably going to trip over someone's feet the first time we all run into the pantry. And how I will likely forget how to cook as soon as the timer starts." She paused to laugh a little at herself. "A veritable parade of positive thinking, right here."

Dahlia pointed to her head. Attempted a charming smile.

Strawberry Blonde Hair blinked.

"Cool, okay, so, great. Good talk. Bye."

Dahlia was beginning to pivot around their shoulder right as a pale hand landed on Dahlia's arm.

"This way, honey."

Oh, thank the goddesses above. Producer Janet was saving Dahlia from herself. Although maybe it was actually too late for that.

As they walked away, to her shock, she actually thought she heard Strawberry Blonde Hair say goodbye.

Dahlia tried to take it all in, as Janet led her through the curving maze of cooking stations that took up the majority of the floor space in the cavernous set. But mainly all she could focus on was how much she liked the bright red frames of Janet's glasses, and the small pulse of warmth that had pushed into her pounding heart when Janet called her *honey*.

They stopped at the very front of the semi-circle of stations, all the way to the right.

"Here you go, Miss Woodson. This is you."

And with a reassuring smile, Janet whirled away to direct the next contestant.

Here were all the details Dahlia had seen on TV for the last seven seasons of Chef's Special: the deep greens and golds and sparkling turquoise scattered throughout the set in pops of colored glass. How the dark wood of the walls and the floor contrasted against those lighter hues.

She had always thought the set resembled an old Scottish castle on the moors, only recently paid a visit by Queer Eye. Cozy and strong all at once, its foundations invoking a sense of time and honor—and here and there, some playful splashes of dazzle.

Dahlia stared down at the shining, stainless steel countertop of her station. *Her* station. Remembering the blank look on Strawberry Blonde's face a few minutes ago, as she made a fool of herself within minutes of stepping onto set, she resisted the urge to lean over and smack her forehead against that stainless steel a few times.

Instead, she closed her eyes and breathed in through her nose, like that yoga class she went to once a year ago had taught her.

Onions. The scraggly brown bits on the top and bottom. The pure whiteness of the insides, firm yet pliant. The reliable structure of layers. So many recipes started with the basic building block of a finely diced onion.

Dahlia was learning, in her new life, to take things one step at a time. If she started with basic building blocks, focused on each small step, she could accomplish things.

Dahlia's eyes blinked open as a tall white man with dark hair ambled over to the workspace next to hers. He was looking down, furiously scribbling in a small notepad. Oh, god. People were taking notes, and Dahlia felt like she'd barely heard half of the words coming out of Janet's mouth this morning. And Janet was loud.

"Hey," the tall dude said, finally looking up. He stuck his pencil behind his ear, all cool like, and held out a thick hand. "Jacob. Looks like we're tablemates."

Dahlia shook his hand. She thought she maybe said her name. She was thrown by how confident he seemed, when all she could think about, aside from onions and that embarrassing scene under the archway, was how gassy she suddenly was. Her stomach was making alarming gurgling sounds. She glanced around the room. All the other contestants were making idle chatter, smiling at each other.

They ranged from cocky and attractive looking, like Jacob, to a short older woman in the opposite corner, her salt and pepper bob shaking as she nodded vigorously at the Black woman next to her.

Wait. Dahlia recognized that bob. She had met that bob on the shuttle to the hotel from the airport two days ago. She was a grandma from Iowa, Dahlia remembered now, and she was exactly what you would expect from a Midwestern grandma: kind, but sharp. Like you knew she made a mean apple pie, but also wouldn't let you get away with any of your shit. Dahlia had loved her immediately. Barbara! That was her name.

A small spark burst to life in Dahlia's veins.

If Barbara could do this, so could she.

But when Dahlia's eyes glided away from Barbara, everyone else's faces blurred at the edges.

She took another deep breath. Peppers. She liked chopping peppers too. Not as satisfying as an onion, but so aesthetically pleasing. Exquisite, vibrant colors, colors that were almost hard to imagine emerging from nothing but seeds, sunshine, dirt.

All you needed were building blocks.

"Hello, contestants of Season Eight!"

Dahlia swiveled back around.

Holy leapin' lizards.

Sai Patel. Sai Patel was in front of her. Standing in the middle of the Golden Circle, where the contestants would be called at the end of each Elimination Challenge to greet their glory or their doom. Dahlia was suddenly disconcerted, even more than she had been a second ago, that her cooking station was so close to this circle, this space which would spike her anxiety and determine her future. It would, in fact, never escape her vision.

Everything was fine.

"I know how nervous you are right now." Bless Sai Patel, and his dark mussed hair, and his shirt with the top button unbuttoned, for saying this out loud. "But remember—we chose you, out of thousands of possible contestants, for a reason. You've already gotten through the hardest part. You're here! And now? This is when the fun starts."

As Sai Patel grinned out at the thirteen contestants of Season Eight, Dahlia could see with her very own eyes that one slightly crooked canine she had observed so many times from the comfort of her couch back in Maryland. It was even more perfect in person, Sai Patel's smile, and the fact that one of the most famous chefs in the world was standing in front of her, appearing genuine and encouraging and fully invested in this whole thing, began to soothe Dahlia's nerves.

He was right, after all. She had made it through the auditions in Philly for a reason. Chef's Special was for amateur chefs; thousands of people tried out each year. It meant something, that she had been one of the thirteen out of all those thousands to make it here. She had worked hard. Her new tablemate Jacob and his dumb pencil behind his ear weren't any better than her. She could do this.

She could win $100,000.

~

ABOUT ANITA KELLY

Originally from a small town in the Pocono Mountains of Pennsylvania, Anita Kelly now lives in the Pacific Northwest with their wife, kiddo, three-legged dog, and scarily affectionate cat. A librarian by day, they spend any time not reading or writing drinking too much tea, taking pictures, and dreaming of their next walk in the woods. They hope you get to pet a dog today.

ALSO BY ANITA KELLY

Full-Length Novels

Love & Other Disasters (out January 2022)

Moonlighters novellas

Sing Anyway

Our Favorite Songs (out Fall 2021)

Made in the USA
Middletown, DE
07 September 2021

47810848R00083